Sci-Fi/Fantasy - PORTR-PTG
TCHAI
Tchaikovsky, Adrian
Ogres
33410017474307   03-31-2022

ONE OF 2000 LIMITED EDITION COPIES

OGRES

ADRIAN TCHAIKOVSKY

First published 2022 by Solaris
an imprint of Rebellion Publishing Ltd,
Riverside House, Osney Mead,
Oxford, OX2 0ES, UK

www.solarisbooks.com

ISBN: 978-1-78618-528-0

Copyright © 2022 Adrian Czajkowski

The right of the author to be identified as the author of this work has been asserted in accordance with the Copyright, Designs and Patents Act 1988.

All rights reserved. No part of this publication may be reproduced, stored in a retrieval system, or transmitted, in any form or by any means, electronic, mechanical, photocopying, recording or otherwise, without the prior permission of the copyright owners.

This book is a work of fiction. Names, characters, places and incidents are products of the author's imagination or are used fictitiously.

10 9 8 7 6 5 4 3 2 1

A CIP catalogue record for this book is available from the British Library.

Designed & typeset by Rebellion Publishing

Printed in the UK

OGRES

CHAPTER ONE

You were always trouble.

Inevitable, really. And you weren't to know it, but you were following a particular trajectory. The Young Prince *is* always trouble. A youth, misspent in bad company and oafish pranks, who can mend their ways when adulthood comes rapping at the door, is more prized than any number of young paragons. People remember, but fondly. *He was always trouble*, they think, shaking their heads and smiling a little. *But look at him now.*

Look at you then, Torquell, the miscreant. You're hiding out because of your latest misdemeanour. Let's say this time it was the apples you couldn't resist, hanging so low on the bough in your neighbour's orchard. So, you and a couple of the boys who would always dog your footsteps were over that stone wall and filling the hollow of your smocks with fruit. And then the neighbour – not, after all, out bartering for eggs as you thought – caught sight of you out of her cottage window. Came out waving her stick and hollering fit to murder the lot of you, and you were over the wall and gone with your treasure. And the others had some feeble attempt at disguise, hoods up, broad-brimmed hats on, a scarf up past the nose despite the muggy heat of early autumn. But the downside of being the village's lovable rogue is that everyone always recognises you. You stand out in a crowd, after all, almost a head over the tallest of your reprobate cronies. And so you've gone to ground to go eat apples and kick your heels; to prepare your well-worn apologies before going to present yourself to your father and face the music. And you'll be made to go apologise, you know. You'll have some chore to do, in punishment. The village elders will shake their heads again and *tsk* through their teeth. But fondly, always fondly. They were young once, and you serve as a kind of magnified memory of all the trouble they never quite got up to but wish they had.

Right now, you're in the forest, because you know nobody will follow you there.

There are outlaws in the forest. Only a handful because the bounties of nature can't support many. Only so many meals in nettles and acorns, after all. Only a handful, too, because the Landlord has stocked the place with boar and deer, and while the latter are merely competition for edibles, the former are a real hazard. But there remains a determined little band of those whose villainies were too great for the fond boys-will-be-boys indulgence your own delinquencies inspired. Men and women who had a rare spark of anger to them, or who just couldn't live with their neighbours. One or two who, it was said, had done something truly awful, though usually those went further than the wood. Because the Landlord is always looking for an excuse to hunt something more interesting than boar. It's said those murderers who get tracked and caught are taken back to the Landlord's estates for another hunt, released into the grounds, and given a head-start before the dogs. The Masters do love their sport.

But none of that for you. You're not a villain, only a charming rogue. Nobody's going to give you up to the Landlord's justice for a few apples.

The leader of the outlaws in the wood is called Roben. And yes, he wears a hood, but only because the canopy isn't quite enough to keep the rain off. You and he have been thick as thieves for years, despite the fact your father's the village headman. Because, of course, he is. You're the young prince in miniature, after all. Although 'miniature' probably isn't quite the word for you. So yes, you keep bad company. Many's the time you've shirked chores or dodged justice to hide out in the woods with Roben and his constantly-changing cast of bad 'uns. Right now there are seven of them, and you're sharing the apples round the fire. Roben's lot are a starveling band, ragged in whatever clothes they have on their backs or have been able to steal. Some of them likely won't survive the winter. A merry greenwood fire is only romantic if you have a roof to go back to. They'll come out of the woods when the frosts start, and hope to find some sheep to share warmth with in a byre somewhere; perhaps a hayloft or a crofter's hut or some other retreat where they won't be discovered till spring begins to massage the world again. But right now your apples are welcome, and they tell tales around the fire: lies about what they did to get them thrown out, tall stories of far villages and further sights. The excesses of the Masters in their great lumbering revels. And you're one of them for as long as you care to share their fire, and then, towards evening, you make ready to go back and face the music. Unlike Roben, you, at least, have a bed and a roof waiting for you.

And you'd think they'd resent you, these outlaws. You'd think they'd hate you, for being the son of the man who's supposed to bring them to justice; for having everything they don't have. But somehow you're their surrogate son, too. And the apples were welcome.

"Bring me a good shirt when you come again, young Torquell," Roben jokes. "Bring me one of your cast-offs, even. I'll use it as a tent." For he's a scarecrow of a man, having survived seven winters in the forest, and you are the enviable prime of youth grown into a man's strength. Half a head, even a full head taller than the strongest of your peers. And, though you do have a temper on you, not a giant's strength used as a giant might but responsibly. Always happy to flex your muscles to lift a cart when it needs a new wheel, to carry a full barrel or fetch water.

Not, in short, an ogre's strength, forever awaiting a victim. Such displays are the prerogative of the Masters, which nobody dares usurp.

And even as you're preparing to depart Roben's company, the cry goes up that there's traffic on the road.

For a moment you see Roben's eye light up with larcenous speculation. All who travel between the villages run the risk of having a certain tax imposed on them, and the likelihood of taxation and the severity of the duties imposed are entirely dependent on how many mouths Roben has to feed and just how hungry they are. They are, after all, outlaws. But the watchman has more to shout, because this traveller's no peddler or merchant come from some other village to barter their surplus. It's no journeyman artisan who might part with a few examples of their work or even mend a boot or stitch that shirt, in exchange for being allowed to progress without a beating. And the stories the robbers tell of their exploits always have the traveller feasting at their greenwood fire, but you know that's mostly wishful thinking. Any such traveller likely carries better vittles than Roben's people could ever lay out, and any such feast would be entirely under duress. But so the stories go, and you prefer them. Already you're starting to see the world in a certain way, with that overlay people paint where desperation and necessity get gilded over into stories.

But these travellers aren't the sort to be subject to Roben's customs duties. The messenger – a scrawny woman out gathering firewood – gabbles the rest of the tale. No human wayfarer this, but ogres and their retinue, headed for the village. The Landlord is making his visit, to see what the harvest will bring. To have his people assess tithes, that he might take his lion's share. Every field and tree, every herd and flock; the real tax that Roben's petty brigandage is a pale imitation of. And under no circumstances would Roben even tell a tall story about standing before an ogre and calling out his stand-and-deliver. The outlaws melt deeper into the trees, away from the road, so that not even the rumble of the Landlord's motorcade can disturb their fitful sleep. And you, young hellion that you are, must hotfoot it back to the village because your father will want you to hand, to greet the Master. The whole village must be there, and you cannot give him the shame of an absent son in the unlikely event the Landlord asks after you. You are trouble, yes; you are the great loutish rogue forever making a nuisance of yourself, and everyone in the village has a story of how you stole or trespassed, tricked or swindled. But fondly, and forgiven after the heat has cooled and fitting penance has been performed. The Masters do not forgive, and they are not fond. Even you know well enough not to offend them. Or you thought you did.

And, because you're you, you go and spy out the ogres as they come to your village.

You don't see them in person as they pass through the woods. Without a retinue to slow them down you'd never outpace them through the trees. The windows are smoked glass. The machine itself is dark metal. The wheels are huge, great rugged tyres of black rubber stippled with studs like knuckles for traction. It's part of the village's due to keep these tracks through the forest clear. Once every two months, everyone strong enough goes out with axe and saw and hacks back any new growth. Others bring in dirt to fill in holes. The children stamp the ground flat after. It's almost like a celebration, everyone coming together for the good of your Masters. And you know what? It rankled with you, even then. Even though your father was keen to impress on you how the world worked from the start. Even though everyone blesses the Masters and thanks the Masters for their protection and cheers when the Landlord comes to your village to take his due. And maybe you heard, a few times, some muttering in back rooms. Or maybe you listened to Roben and his people, glorifying their freedom from the yoke as they starved and froze out in the woods. But maybe it was within you from the start. Maybe that's what made you a hero.

Right now, the first incident in that hero's journey is waiting just past the horizon and you have no idea, no idea at all.

The Landlord's car growls on over the track, which is still rugged with roots and potholes despite the village's best efforts. A second car behind holds the Landlord's most favoured servants. There will be some inside the enclosed cab, but on the flatbed back are his beaters, a quartet of humans trusted enough to be given clubs. And everyone knows the Masters don't *need* people to protect them. Who'd be the fool to lift a hand against an ogre, even if they were so misguided as to resent the way things were?

But sometimes the Landlord will want justice done, a transgression punished, and will not want to soil his own huge hands. Hence the beaters.

Also laid out on the flatbed, two corpses. The Landlord has been indulging himself on his way over. Deer, of course. Why else stock the woods with them, if not to take out a rifle and re-establish the old ogrish supremacy over nature? A doe and a buck, bloody where the shot went in. The Landlord is bringing the makings of his own feast.

And a score of other servants, walking alongside or riding ponies. You've often wondered what that would be like. They're huge beasts, those ponies, though not the size of the horses an ogre would ride. Ogre children train on them, you're told, but a grown ogre adult would break the poor things' backs. And the human riders are muffled up to sweltering point: heavy gloves, heavy britches to ward off a rash from the animal's bristling hide. Only an ogre can stroke that gleaming roan flank with bare-handed impunity.

The sound of the engine will have alerted your father and all the village, and you vaguely remember your old dad telling you the visit is expected. It's harvest time, after all, and so cometh all the business of taxes and assessment. A good year for the village means full pockets for the Landlord. It's his village, after all. Your father, the headman, is just managing it for him, taking responsibility for whatever goes wrong. He's tried to impose upon you the serious burden of the work given that it'll pass to you in time. But you're not the serious type. He despairs of you.

Not the serious type *yet*.

And they're all lined up to welcome the Landlord by the time the motorcade and retinue arrive. Your ogrish Master drives slowly between the houses of his subjects, the top of his car level with the sills of their upper-storey windows, and everyone cheers. Children have been given flower garlands hastily woven. The hands have been called in from the fields. Everyone has done their utmost to get into their Sunday best clothes, their churchgoing finest. And your father stands there front and centre of the throng looking desperately worried because his delinquent son is nowhere to be seen.

But you're the lovable rogue with perfect timing, and you can put a sprint on when you choose. So, just as the car is drawing up, just as the ponies are being reined in, you're there at his side. Even shrugging into a clean shirt, your face half-washed. The old woman who does your father's laundry tuts and spits into a hankie, cleans away the last smudge of trail dust, and then it's all faces front. Everyone cheers. Hooray for the ogres.

Servants bustle to open the car door – two of them, to haul it all the way – and a gust of cool air wafts from inside the vehicle. That ogre magic, just like the motive force that makes the car engine growl into life. Because they can do anything, the ogres. Sorcerers, so say the people. God's chosen, so says the pastor. The might of the ogres isn't solely contained in their great limbs and strength.

But that is what strikes the eye, when you see them. You, big and strong for a man, are used to weighing others by the amount of world they displace and the force they can exert. And when the Landlord, Sir Peter Grimes, gets out of the car, you cannot but judge him a great power in the world. If you are over six feet tall and your father five and a half, then Sir Peter is ten, easily. And vast, a great tun of a body, thick-waisted and heavy. A flat face that would look human if it weren't so big that it becomes just a great, jowly topography. The eyes seemingly squeezed half shut by the opposing pressure of cheeks and brow, though perhaps that's just against the brightness of the light outside of the car. And such clothes! Casual travel wear to an ogre puts all your village finery to shame. Such fabrics and shines, so silky and flowing that no loom could possibly have woven them! Such colours: slate grey and red-burgundy and gold. And when everyone bows before him, perhaps it's a relief. To have an excuse to take your eyes away from such opulence and such a vast mass of flesh standing there on two pillar legs.

"Tomas, as I live and breathe!" booms Sir Peter. "Come forward, Tomas. I trust the accounts are all prepared? You've taken census already?" Because when the Landlord calls, he expects to find everything in order. And it isn't just a matter of the village lined up and the children running forward with their garlands – all fielded by the servants who'll dispose of them later because the ogres can't be expected to deal with such things. It's a matter of having it all writ down, each bushel and basket, every laying hen, each of the hulking sheep counted on the hillside, every cow in the pasture. And woe betide the headman who cheats his Landlord, or even miscounts. There's always someone who will slip the word in some servant's ear, for preferment or for their children's advancement. A headman takes responsibility, your father tells you often, and there will somehow always be someone who feels that responsibility should be theirs.

But the village can't show that side of its dealings to the Masters, obviously, and so it's all cheering and garlands as Tomas, your father, smiles and assures Sir Peter that all is well. And inwardly, no doubt, he's fretting, because though the pastor taught you letters and numbers, it's a side of your duties you've shown no keenness for, and time doth march on. It would be no great consolation to him, of course, if he were to look into the future and see how hard you'll work at it in due course.

And then Sir Peter turns back and helps another ogre out of the car. This one is almost as tall but less grown into his bulk. A youth, perhaps no more than your own eighteen years. He has a face that's handsome, in the way that ogres often are before time and excess fill them out and cruelty engraves them. Except cruelty is already there on this giant lad's features and you mark it well. He looks over the gathering, all the people of your village, meaning most of the people you have ever met in your life. His expression can be best summed up as contempt. No attempt to disguise the curl of the lip, the incredulous *is-this-it?* of him. He's seen a dozen villages already on this little pilgrimage, and yours is nothing special. Sir Peter has dragged him from his estates and his ogrish pleasures for *this*.

"My son, Gerald," Sir Peter says, clapping the boy on the

broad shoulder with a sound like thunder. "He'll be taking over from me in time. Thought I'd show him how it's done. Let him see who he'll be dealing with. And this is your own, unless I miss my guess." And a sizing up, then, because you are nine inches closer to his eye level than your father ever was, with perhaps a little growth left in you still. "Quite the figure he cuts," says Sir Peter, his eyes twinkling in their deep nests. Even in good humour his face can't quite iron out all those hard lines. And he is in good humour too. He doesn't register the sour, sulky look of young Gerald. He's doing his father-and-son-time bit, the lord-of-all-he-surveys patter, the benign dictator with absolute power of life and death over everyone and everything within a long ride of his house.

"A likely lad," Sir Peter proclaims you. "Mark him, Gerald. He'll be headman of the village, I'd guess, by the time I hand the business over to you. He'll serve you well, I don't doubt." All colossal joviality is Sir Peter Grimes right then. But Gerald is not. Gerald is bored and resentful, and you're put in front of him, and perhaps you become a stand-in for all the things provoking his ill humours then, and perhaps that's what contributes to what comes later.

THERE WILL BE a feast, of course. The village opens its barns and larders so that Sir Peter can have his pick of all the good things. Everyone who's a proven cook will pitch in, and your father's house will overflow with guests as Sir Peter gets his knees under your groaning table. Everything that can be done with bread and vegetables and fruit, milk, eggs, and honey, will be carried out and set before the ravenous appetites of the pair of ogres. But ogres require more and different sustenance than regular humans, of course. No call to kill the fatted calf or have four men haul in a protesting sheep for the knife, though. Sir Peter has provided for himself with his hunting trip. You watch as the two stiff carcasses of the deer are manhandled off the flatbed by the gloved hands of the beaters. Curious, because you've not seen such a thing often, you follow them in to your father's kitchen. A big kitchen, in the village's biggest house, but right now it's cluttered and you're an extra body, a big lad taking up room.

Sir Peter's chef is just a human, of course. There's no crossover between the Masters and mere servants. He's a plump little man, dressed in finer clothes than you've ever worn, now tying an apron about his waist and shouting at a half dozen other culinary servants. Your father's kitchen has become occupied territory. At the far end, the house's cook and maid are penned, trying to deal with their part of the feast in a cupboard's worth of space as the strangers take over. The rest of the feast – ogrish appetites being what they are – is being cooked up across the village, everyone doing their bit. But here, the chef is in command, and he'll brook no challenge to his minuscule authority.

And you might just have ducked out, gone round the front way to get into your own house, but it irks you. That this dressed-up dandy can swan in and colonise your home, no matter that he has the Landlord's writ about him.

You always did have a temper, and a sense of injustice. While your father, as headman, heard complaints and made judgments under the sun, you had your own practices under the moon. When you knew some malefactor, greedy or cruel, who'd escaped accusation or wormed their way out of public show, you'd find some way to even the score. A little vandalism, a little theft, some prank that would, at least, humiliate them. For all you're a big lad, you can be subtle too, and you were always good at talking your peers into helping out. A troublemaker, but even when you yourself were up before your father, somehow everyone understood the good heart behind the rash actions. Perhaps that should have gone first in the litany of *things that make you what you become*. You always got away with it, before.

And so you go into the kitchen where the chef squawks and upbraids, and you pause to see how they skin and gut the deer, gloved hands working as fast and dextrously as they can, and the blood mopped off any bare skin before it can raise a rash. And then one of the cooks backs into you and drops a pan and the chef rounds on you. Your burly build does not intimidate him for one moment, little master, as he is, of all he surveys. "Out, you oaf! You peasant!" he shrieks, and you're laughing at him even then, already about to slouch out of the kitchen and find your father. But he's not done asserting his authority, and the laughter doesn't help, and he strikes you with the big wooden spoon he's been wielding like a sceptre. One, two, across the arm, and you barely feel it through your shirt. And even you recognise that your grin is a bit oafish by then, enjoying yourself too much. And then he hits you across the face with the spoon's edge, right in the eye.

Your temper flares, and you take the spoon from him and break it across your knee. The kitchen goes very quiet.

"This is my house," you tell the man. "You'll keep a civil tongue, when you speak to me or mine" – and you're taking on yourself your father's office, whether or not you're entitled to it. You remember Sir Peter talking about you filling your father's shoes, and perhaps that went to your head just a little.

And then Gerald is there.

You don't know why the Landlord's son is in the kitchen. Perhaps he's used to scrounging scraps from the servants like you, though likely with menaces rather than a winning smile. He has stooped in through the back door, ducking low and feeding his shoulders in sideways. Now he can't quite stand straight, head canted forwards under the human-scale ceiling. The ogre boy, looking from the chef to you.

"Castor, what's the problem?" His voice is a purr. He's already looked ahead and seen some fun to be had.

The chef stammers, and if you were sharper you'd see how very frightened he suddenly is, because you don't come to the attention of the ogres unless you're very sure no blame can possibly alight on you. "Master, this man, this man…" A trembling spasm of fingers towards you. "It is impossible to work while my kitchen is disrupted by such…"

Gerald Grimes lurches over, looming, grinning. And you were grinning at Castor earlier, sure enough, but your face never held this kind of malice. And perhaps there is a spark of commonality between you, ogre and human though you are. The difference is mostly that enough hands were on you in your childhood to temper your wilfulness. Gerald Grimes was only ever subject to Sir Peter. Other than that, his birthright was lordship of all creation.

But perhaps he senses that you are like him, just a little – some version of him not corrupted by the power he was born to, and perhaps that's why he decides to make you regret it.

"The headman's son," he says. And then, in a parody of his own father's voice, "Quite the figure he cuts. A likely lad. It's you I'll have to thank, is it, when I have to drag myself from cards and hounds to listen to you little monkeys jabber?" And he shoves you. Just a little, the first time. Cooks scuttle out of the way behind as you stagger.

You don't have a ready quip to defuse the situation, and Gerald doesn't want to be defused anyway. He wants to put you in your place. He wants to enact his frustrations after being stuck in a car for days, touring a succession of dreary little villages.

"You impudent little shit," he tells you. "Looking at my father as if your opinion's worth a damn. I should have the beaters whip you, out in the square where everyone can see." And you weren't looking at his father and he's not even using your contretemps with Castor as a *casus belli*. It's just him being fed up and wanting to let his temper off the leash, and you made yourself a target. And he shoves you harder, all that solid ogre strength, the sheer brute force of a man three feet taller and far heavier than you.

"Castor," he says, "have one of your monkeys fetch a whip. I'll show golden boy here just how it's going to be when we're both in our fathers' shoes."

The third shove comes in, slamming you against a wall, spilling pots and pans off a shelf with your elbow, and your temper finally finds its breaking point and you punch him in the jaw. And yes, he was hunched forwards so that jaw was very invitingly presented. Off-balance, perhaps, from pushing you. Mind so full of the thought of wielding the whip that he wasn't considering you might fight back. People don't, after all. Not against the Masters.

And he goes down with a roar, crashing back into the gore of the gutted deer, spilling bowls of blood, jugs of milk, scattering Castor and his minions like pins. And you've struck an ogre. You've struck a Master. You've done the thing no human may do.

For a moment the world is as horrified as you, frozen and aghast, and in that moment you flee from the kitchen, running like a child to find your father and confess to what you've done.

CHAPTER TWO

You brace yourself for the slap in return. From your father it wouldn't hurt your body, but it could still hurt inside. You love the old man, for all you seem to spend your every day exasperating him. Instead he goes very still. You've come to him in his own room where some of the neighbours are dressing him, all the finest clothes never brought out for less than a feast day, and still not a patch on Sir Peter's garments. He orders everyone out. The news will be all over the village in minutes. *Torquell struck the Landlord's son!* Horror, shame, and yet (you think) perhaps a little thread of sneaking admiration. It's what you're used to, from your most daring exploits. Everyone loves to shake their head and tut over your escapades, but you've coasted through life this far on a frictionless layer of *Ah, youth!*

and *I remember when I was his age…*

But there's none of that in your father's eye right now. "You have to leave," he says, and his voice is so bleak you think for a heart-stopping moment that he means *forever*. But his mind is still working, his mouth still turning out the words one by one as his brain mints them. "For this evening, just get out of the village. I know you take yourself off into the trees to share a fire with those villains out there. Go do that, now." Your father, the headman, recommending you to the company of outlaws. "Don't come back until well after dark. Until morning, would be even better. I'll speak with Sir Peter. I'll square things with him. You just put yourself out of sight." He isn't berating you, telling you what a fool you are, what a lout. Not a word of the usual catechism about controlling your temper, about thinking ahead over the consequences of what you do. That scares you most of all. You're braced for a bawling-out, for him to shout in his reedy voice, for him to take up his stick and strike you. You'd welcome, right then, the stocks in the village square, public ridicule, honest shame honestly earned. But your father is in full emergency mode, his voice hard and his words hurried, rushing out as though he's dispatching them to the four corners of the village on desperate errands.

And there's no more to it than that, and no more time for anything. Gerald Grimes will have gone to complain to his father, and you must be gone before the Landlord comes with grievances for his tenant.

"I'll make everything right," your father tells you, "but I

can't do it if you're here in his eye. Just go." And you go.

If anyone sees you, you don't note them. No unfamiliar experience, to slip out of the village while you're supposed to be somewhere else; it's part of your stock-in-trade to be absent from your proper place and making mischief elsewhere. You're out past the houses in a blink. Then it's the dykes and the low pastures and the backs of hills, never letting yourself appear stark against the skyline. And, after you've exhausted the bounds of the territory your father holds on Sir Peter's authority, the woods.

There you rest, confident that nobody is on your heels, not from the village, not the beaters nor any from Sir Peter's retinue. You'll find Roben and his people soon enough and spend an hour or so by their fire before you start to slope back, but right then you're not fit for other company. Unusual, for you, whose life has been lived as equal parts cautionary tale and exemplar. You've done a bad thing, though. And not in the usual way – the broken window, the scattered flock, things that time and penance can mend. You've struck an ogre.

They've always been there, your Masters the ogres. All your life and your father's life and your grandfather's and his. Generations of Sir Peter's line have lived on the estate, and there are perhaps fifty villages all tending flocks and tilling fields within the curtilage of their domain. *Their* flocks, *their* fields, on which you and yours are permitted to dwell and work. And of everything the good green earth produces, the ogre's share must come out first, and only hope there's enough left over to feed all the mouths.

And your father and his father have been wise stewards, and there's been no savage pestilence to blacken the fields or lay the hens barren, and so times have been good. You've never known real privation, though the oldsters of the village will tell you of hard times *their* parents knew. And of course, much of what your neighbours tend is for the ogres alone. You have the milk, the eggs, and the wool, but the meat is for the Masters. It is a sermon you've sat fidgeting through often enough, how God has ordered the world. *The Master in his castle,* as the hymn goes, *the poor man at the gate.* So it is that God gave unto the ogres the rule of all the world, and placed the beasts, tame and wild, in it for their sole pleasure. No human constitution could stomach that venison Sir Peter brought with him, nor a flank of mutton or even a leg of fowl. If ever you were tempted to stand up from your pew at church and demand proof that God divides His faithful into high and lowly, that simple fact should be enough to silence you.

You tried, once. Children always do, you suspect. They'd slaughtered sheep for the Landlord's visit and you carved off a bloody lump and took it with a few of your wastrel friends off to a high field. You made a fire between you and you cooked the flesh until it looked the way you'd seen at other occasions when Sir Peter had come to be feasted and collect his tax. By then, those who'd even just handled the flesh had a rash on their hands, but you dared each other until the flesh did the rounds, each of you biting off the least morsel you could get away with. But before the meat even got to you, the first boy was vomiting up his breakfast, and the previous day's breakfast. Then the next followed suit, and so you never did sample the forbidden delicacy of flesh. You just laughed at your fellows, and then took them back to the village, shamefaced and embarrassed, so that Nell Healer could look them over. And all the adults knew what you'd been about, and they shared sly looks that suggested they, too, had tried to test that boundary in their time. But it was and is a boundary, a border between human and ogre. The lowly beasts may eat flesh, and the lofty Masters, but not you. It is, the pastor says, God's will. For if humanity found itself able to eat meat, we would multiply beyond all reason and strip the world bare, not a beast, not a fowl left. We cannot be trusted with such appetites, the pastor says. They are only for our betters.

Out there at the forest's edge you sit and feel sorry for yourself, and the panic and shock of what you did slowly transmutes to resentment, the way it often does. Because, despite your father and despite the pastor, you've always felt a little pang when the Landlord's big car rolls up. When his servants take over your father's house for his comforts. When you're reminded, by the sheer gravity of an ogre's physical presence, that you have *betters*. And was that youth, Gerald, so much more than you, that he could talk to you like that, beard you in your own home? Your anger rises in you, that which you inherited from neither mild parent, not your father, still less the mother you barely recall, dead before you were five years old; too mild to survive the birth of a second child. And again the pastor's dreary sermon trotted out for such circumstances. That women are made to give birth in pain because that is God's plan for them and expiation for leading humanity astray; that to bring new life into the world must necessarily carry with it a risk of death, for otherwise how humanity would swarm across the world and pick it clean. You don't remember the words from your own mother's funeral, but you've heard them plenty since.

And everyone knows the ogres don't suffer from such things, or not as much. They don't get sick like humans do, and should some physical shock prove enough to break even their massive bones, they can be mended like new, so you've heard. Ogre magic; the learning that God allots them, that lets them move their cars without horses and spin thread without wool.

There's a world of ogres out there, so you've heard. Not that you've ever met anyone who's seen it, but fourth-hand and fifth-hand stories confirm it, and you believe. A world of estates and their meek little subject villages, yes, but beyond that, other wonders. Magical ogre castles in the clouds, great gatherings of a hundred hundred humans in one place to do the Masters' bidding. Mountains and seas and other things that perhaps you saw a picture of once, or that the pastor mentioned in his sermons. But you never saw these things, nor did anyone you know, and though you boast and dream, you believe you never will.

And you're wrong. In this one thing your ambitions fall short of the facts of your life. You're a hero in the making after all. Heroes get to do these things. Otherwise, what would there be to write about when their lives are chronicled?

So, eventually, even you tire of your own brooding and go hunting for Roben o' the Wood or any of his people. They see you coming, of course. With Sir Peter in the area, they're extra cautious because the Landlord and his beaters might choose to hunt these woods, and they'll take a brace of outlaws as readily as pheasant or deer. They know you though, and there's no mistaking you for an ogre, nor even one of their minions. Especially when you tell them what you've done.

And the tale grows a little in the telling, it's true. Tales always do. You make the confrontation between you and Gerald Grimes a far grander melee. You become engrossed in your own retelling, a version that has you less the shoved and more the shover. You invent high words from your own lips and more stuttering and spluttering from Gerald's, until the whole band of them is laughing and cheering you on. You strike him not once, but two, three times, heady with your own imagined boldness. The visit to your father goes unmentioned. Not for a defiant hero to go hiding in the parental shadow after all! You came to the woods of your own notion, to hide out with the free fellows before swanning back to town later when heads have cooled.

And Roben, who's been a woodsman and outlaw through many hard winters and therefore is no fool, gets a narrow look on his face as you talk. Of course, he knows you, and he knows your tales. Perhaps at first he reckons that at the heart of this one is a kernel of nothing more than a stumble or a harsh word or an impudent look. Perhaps not, though, as your turn as raconteur runs on. He is used to being the top dog of his outlaw pack, whipped curs as they all are. He hears a hundred lies and arguments a day. He's good at sieving out the truth from words. He hears the truth in yours. Less amused than you anticipated, more fretful. The welcome becomes colder than you expected. They don't laugh like you thought they might. You forget the difference between you sometimes. They're real outlaws. For all they lend a fire when you're skiving from village life and thank you kindly when you bring them eggs or apples or a couple of your father's old jumpers, you're not one of them. More than a foot in the settled and law-abiding world is what they see when they look at you. Oh, they like you, because you're a likeable lad, but they remember you have a roof to go shelter under when it rains.

You'd planned to stay the night with them, shamble home with the dawn, but Roben's stand-offish welcome irritates you, and soon enough you start back from the woods. Overhead, the evening stars are winking open. You watch one of the moving ones, coursing across the sky and gleaming like fire. The ogres put them there, so says the pastor, to watch over all the Earth. But the pastor would tell you the ogres put *everything* in its proper place, people included. They were God's chosen, given the right and the power to order and name everything in creation. So who's to know what's really so?

It's dark by the time you reach the village. Your house is lit up from every window though, and you hear the roar of Sir Peter's revelry, he and his retinue in full feast still. You could stride in the front door and take your place at the table; that's what a hero would do, doubtless. Except you feel equal parts ill-used and miserable and a fool right now, and have no wish to be forced to some punishment or humiliation to make amends. You'll slip in by the kitchen door again, but first you skulk up to the windows to peer inside.

Your family's front room is crowded. The big table's been fully extended and Sir Peter holds ebullient court at the head, looming over all. Gerald hulks beside him, and on his face is a look you recognise from your own attendance at various onerous but unavoidable gatherings. In the leaping light of the hearth you can't see any sign of a bruise, and perhaps that's because of the thick skin of ogres, or because their magics can banish such blemishes. And further down the table are the beaters and the rest of Sir Peter's staff, all riotously tucking in to the end of the meal – just the bread and the vegetable stew and the fruit and such human food. The flesh, the bones that Sir Peter is even now gnawing at, they are for the ogres alone.

And a fine selection of your neighbours, though they mostly seem very subdued, picking at plates barely touched, no conversation between them. Except for Farley Baker, a man your father never could be getting on with, though his is a family too prosperous to exclude from gatherings such as this. Farley sits up close to Sir Peter and guffaws at every ogrish jest.

You don't see your father, but it's late. There are several empty chairs with only the whiff of excuses made to explain them. He does not relish revelry, preferring to do the accounts or read some new ballad sheet or play artless music on his viol.

Time for you to face the music, but you'll do it by degrees. No bursting in like the prodigal for this son. So you sneak round the back of your own house as if you were one of Roben's men for real. You spend a long time waiting by the kitchen door, listening for the sound of any final preparations by Castor, any sweeping up by your nephews or cousins, but there's nothing. Safe, therefore, to creep in, and the door's never barred anyway.

And in you creep, silent as you like, and you're in a familiar kitchen occupied by unfamiliar scents of death. Because nobody prepares meat in here, absent an ogre to feed. The air reeks of blood and, more distantly, of offal. You feel as though you're entering dangerous territory suddenly. You pause by the table and take stock.

A deal of cleaning for someone, and you suspect that might be you, part of your punishment. Well, it's a miserable chore, but you'll do it gladly, if it will expiate a sin or two. No joy to mop up the blood or take out the bones to bury, certainly. You'll need gloves to the elbow and doubtless you'll still end up with weals and red blisters where too much of the charnel remains come into contact with your skin. But these things fade.

Sir Peter's people have brought in two ice boxes, another piece of ogre magic. From one, the buck's head stares glassily up at you through a pale mist of cold air. A trophy for the wall, to join the doubtless hundred others. Sir Peter loves his hunting. You've heard, via Roben, via travellers from other villages, that he's always after importing ever more exotic beasts to his woods. Everyone knows someone who knows someone who heard of a village wiped out by some gigantic long-toothed cat, or a lake no man can fish in because of the crocodiles it was stocked with. But those places are far away and most likely fictitious. Here there is no worse than boar, though a tusked pig that comes up to your shoulder is dangerous enough.

The tabletop is a disarray of bones, those that didn't get served up with the meat. You stare at them dully, feeling your restless gorge try to rise.

Food for ogres, not for men. You never picked apart a roast fowl or watched your father carve a joint. You know death, though, and bones. You grew up on farms. You've seen a lost sheep after the crows have been at it a while. When you were twelve, you and some other kids dug up old Henders' lost calf after it had been in the ground a month, just out of ghoulish curiosity. And one of Roben's men killed a deer last year and boiled its bones and tried to carve them. Gave up because of what it did to the skin of his fingers; but even so, you know bones.

There are ribs, there on the table, and a spine and pelvis. Not the limbs, not the head, but you know. Nothing that wore those bones inside it ever walked on four legs.

And your gaze strays towards the second ice box, the one without the antlers clearing its rim.

Ogres have appetites, everyone knows.

You remember Sir Peter cracking a long bone for its marrow, in your family's front room, at your table. And you remember it a certain way, at variance with the truth. Because, despite the stories children tell each other, ogres don't have tusks and fangs, just bigger teeth than people, to go in their bigger jaws.

And when you jerk away from the table, a whiplash of revelation going through all of you, Gerald is there, ducking low through the door. How did he know you would be here? There's no surprise on his heavy, handsome face. Perhaps it's that you and he are so alike, the disaffected sons of your communities' respective leaders. Rebels who are yet indulged in your little rebellions. The golden boys of very different households. If you'd been born an ogre, you'd be something a bit like Gerald. If he'd been human, he'd be, if not you, then your dark twin: all the same mischiefs but with a heart of cruelty behind them that was never yours. So perhaps you're linked, you and he – he your vast shadow, or you his dwarfish one – and when you stepped back across the threshold, he *knew*.

Or he just saw you peering in through the window. Less mythic, but more rational. Take your pick of explanations.

He's grinning, and when he sees you've just about worked it out, that grin gets so wide you half imagine the top of his head just falling off.

"I bet you thought," he tells you softly, "your father had missed the feast. But never fear, he's there."

Frozen, you stare at him as he pads across the kitchen, looming round the table.

"You see what you did?" he asks you pleasantly. "You *struck* me, boychild." Right in front of you now, filling your whole world, shoulders against the ceiling beams as though one great flex would crack the house in two. "Dad was in two minds, but I said, 'No. Zero tolerance. We can't let the monkeys get away with it. There's only one way to teach them their place.' And since you'd run away like the coward you are, who was left to pay the price but your dear old paterfamilias?" He lingers over the unfamiliar word, its meaning only coming to you from context.

"They said you'd have to move out of the big house. They're making one of the other monkeys headman for now," Gerald says, conversationally. He could snap you in half. You're easily within his long-armed reach. His breath reeks of beer and flesh. You have no strength in you. You've brought all this about. Just like every other occasion you misbehaved, your father has set things right. He's given his all for you, this one last time.

"But I had my father tell them that, give it a couple of years, I want you as headman after all," Gerald almost whispers. Almost like a lover, because he *is* loving it, your stricken expression, his power over you. His revenge. "I want it to be you when I come here on my own for the taxes. I want you to feast me in that room, and bow and scrape. And remember what you did. I want you to smile when you do it."

He's leaning full-length over the table now, his face right in yours and the woodwork groaning with the weight he's putting on it. He's about to tell you to go with him to the front room, to take a seat at the feast. It's not something you could ever do. And that smile just keeps getting wider, and perhaps that serves as the final spark.

Your temper, which had been doused ashes through all of this, is abruptly aflame like never before. You shake. You see red. It's not even a need for familial vengeance that moves you. It's the shame. It's your own self-condemnation. Action is the only way you can even start to erase it. You, the meagre human, the village boy; him, the Landlord's son, the ogre. He could snap you like kindling in those huge hands.

But those huge hands are on the table, and his weight is on them. No sudden moves from him, all out of balance as he is. And Castor the chef has left the tools of his trade scattered about for his minions to clear up after the feast.

In the midst of your father's ruined ribs is a cleaver, and at once you have it up and buried in Gerald's face with all your might. And Castor keeps an edge on that steel; even after a day of hacking bones it's razor keen. The ogre youth rips back his head and gives out a muted sound for all the world like an ox in pain and you have the gleaming blade drawn back and the second slice cuts him a new smile even broader than the first, ear to ear across that conveniently bared throat.

And then you are gone, fleeing the charnel kitchen, fleeing the house, the village, running for the woods with blood in your eyes and on your hands.

CHAPTER THREE

THEY AREN'T EXPECTING to see you again so soon, Roben's people, still less so bloody and in such disarray. You'd run all the way to the treeline. And right then there isn't any will in you to dissemble. You are stripped down to the bones of who you were. What came from your mouth was more confession than anything else. The ogres had killed your father. Your actions had killed your father. You had killed an ogre.

Stunned silence from them. And then… a medley of reactions; quite the range, now you think back on it. Because some still have that core in them, hammered there by church and village life before they did whatever each one did to make them outlaw. Some are shocked that you could even lift a hand against the Masters, let alone shed so much of that vast reservoir of blood that it might kill one. Taboos like that, beat into you from earliest childhood, they don't get shaken free so easily. Garett, the oldest of them, is pale and shaking his head, and Nell Wilso sucks at her toothless gums. But some of the others, their eyes are lit up. They're the ones whose crimes were against the property, not of humans but of ogres. They lost that reverence, and maybe they've dreamed of doing just what you did every night since. And right then you're in no position to appreciate it, lost in a welter of guilt and panic, but it's the first time people look at you like that. Not fond, not exasperated. You're not the prodigal son or the lovable rogue right then. You're the hero who slays the monster.

"Serves the fucker right," says Manx Jack, one of the youngest and most bitter of the outlaws. "We should go there right now and do for the da what he did to the son. Show the fuckers right, we should."

But that is a step nobody else feels up to taking. Plenty of tales of gallant have-nots striking against those who still *have*, be they corrupt humans or the ogres themselves. But this band of ne'er-do-wells never went further than larceny, and that only around the frayed edges of a village's life. And even the tales don't go as far as seeing ogre blood on the floor. At least, not until this moment.

"Pack up everything that's worth it," Roben decides then. "We're moving, right now."

There's a chorus of complaint at that, but he speaks over them.

"Critch Hollow. We'd be headed there soon enough anyway, to winter over. It's no great hardship to bring the trip forwards. Garett, you're still friendly with the Widow Neris there, aren't you?"

"If she's still living," the old man admits.

"Then let's hope she is, for it's like to be a bitter winter. But we move now, because they'll have every man and woman searching the woods for Torquell before dawn and we cannot be here."

And your head was full of your own problems, and you never thought of that. In coming to Roben, you've daubed every one of his band with the red of what you did. Should Sir Peter and his beaters come, with a mob riled up from the village, how would they be treated? Hanged from the trees that were their shelter, every one of them. Another lance of guilt to ram into your innards. But Roben is all business, kicking and sweet-talking his people in turn until they're all in motion, gathering their blankets and bedrolls and makeshift tents, what food they've not eaten, what spare clothes they've scrounged from washing lines and out of untended windows.

And you stand there, at the periphery of all this activity, head still churning like a sick stomach, unable to think straight. You vomited the story right up for them, and yet it's still inside you. And you realise it always will be, and you'll always feel like this when you think on it. You've made a new part of yourself tonight, forged red hot in anger and then pressed to your flesh until it's melted its way to your bones.

And then Roben looks at you and says, "Well come on, then."

Later, you understand what a grand thing that is for him to say. That despite the lack of it in his face, he was more of Manx Jack's mind than old Garett's or Nell Wilso's. "You've earned your outlawry, boy," he says. "You need no prating elder to tell you you've no place in a village anymore. And you know full well it's a hard bastard life, but what've you got else?" And the expressions on the others are that same mixed bag, but none of them is going to gainsay Roben right then. And it's as simple as that, how you became an outlaw. One of a variety of skins you'll wear throughout your life.

AND YOU HAVE no blanket or bedroll, though at least your clothes have fewer holes than theirs. But you have strong arms, and despite your usual high opinion of yourself – currently overturned, but it'll be back – you've never been averse to using them to help others. You carry a big stack of firewood over your shoulder, and you carry the pack of whoever's most in need of it. You make yourself useful, because right then you have a dire need to do anything that will shave away at the gnawing guilt inside you. And some nights on that trip, your dreams find you back in the kitchen. And some nights, in dreams, you not only see the all-too-human bones, but look into that second ice box too. And your father's face looks back. Another trophy for Sir Peter's wall to go with the bucks and the boars.

Sometimes you whimper half the night, and once or twice you wake screaming and thrashing and trying to kill Gerald all over again. But you're not the only one of the band who has memories that won't go away, and the others curse you and cuff you but only half-heartedly. And the travel is hard, through the woods and off the tracks, and a lot of the time you're so tired that the dreams can't get to you at all.

Critch Hollow is a place you visited once with your father, when you were much smaller. You remember the journey, by ox-cart and with a whole delegation of villagers. Someone was getting wed, some girl of your parish. You remember good food and dancing and getting to stay up late. Critch Hollow as an outlaw is nowhere near as fun, and by the time Roben's band takes up residence in the nearby woods, the first sniff of frost is in the air. A hard winter, he says, and he's been at this life long enough to know.

The salvation of the band is the Widow Neris, still very much alive. She's a tough old bird living on the far outskirts of Critch with a daughter and a granddaughter and a couple of foundling girls she's taken in. And there's precious little *frail* in that *old*, and the girls are all broad-backed and strong-armed from farm work, and if Roben's band intended mischief it would be an even match, you reckon. The Widow Neris does indeed have a soft spot for old Garett, though, and a warm bed for him too. The outlaws get a haybarn to hide out in, and they earn their keep in what has obviously become an annual tradition. They never told you about this side of the life, around the greenwood fire near your home. Not exactly thumbing their noses at authority and living free in the forest. Not that you're complaining. Roben says snow's on the way, and a haybarn seems a fine thing to have the loan of after that news.

And you work. All of you work, with more or less enthusiasm. And as the largest and the strongest – and, until very recently, the best fed – you work the hardest, fetching water and wood, mending what's broken, painting what's peeled. And the Widow Neris lives far enough from any other stead and has enough feuds with all her neighbours that nobody comes calling to see how she's doing. Only her daughter and one of the foundling girls take a little cart into Critch every few days, the child being more personable than the mother. They come back with news and made-goods that Neris needs but can't craft herself, bartered for with bundles of firewood and medicinal herbs and trays of eggs from Neris's fine hens.

And you heal. Time gives you a month to heal before upsetting the course of your life again. Something of the old You comes back. The outlaws have taken to you because you don't shirk and because you start to put that lovable rogue act back on. One of Neris's foundlings is sweet on you, too, but the Widow has a hard rule about that kind of thing. No swelling bellies is her agreement with Roben, and he's made sure everyone understands it. Old Garret, who has his, cackles at the rest of you and tells unlikely tales of his nocturnal acrobatics and the Widow's appetites. And Manx Jack gets you on your own once, and tries to get you to go against Roben and go with the girl, willing as she is. He wants the vicarious thrill of it, you reckon, or else he thinks he might be next to get lucky once you've leant your weight against that forbiddance and weakened it. And, even though you've had some longing thoughts of a warm bed of your own, you tell him one warm night now isn't worth freezing out in the woods next winter.

And it is a hard winter, just like Roben says, and the snow comes early and won't leave. And firewood's still very much required, and so you and the strongest of both the outlaws and of Neris's brood all go your ways into the trees to gather what the canopy has left dry enough while the white clouds hold off, because nobody wants to run out in the middle of the next storm.

One time, already cold and hungry, the snow catches you, and you're trapped beneath the tree-shadow because it's a long walk across exposed fields to get back to the barn. You had no breakfast, and you've had no lunch, and by nightfall you've a hollow pit where your stomach was. You find a stream but it's iced over to the stones of its belly so you can't even fill your guts with chill water. And then you find the deer.

A young deer, this year's, and going nowhere. Skidded on the ice, you reckon, and its leg is broken hard enough for the bones to show through its skin. When you take up a stick, it's mostly out of pity. You crack its skull on the second swing, and that's all the mercy this world has for a deer with broken legs.

Perhaps it's the sight of the raw, exposed bone that sets the thought on you, but you build a fire next, all the wood you'd gathered repurposed for your own immediate survival. You've enough woodcraft that you pick a good hollow where the warmth will linger, and you bank up snow and fallen needles on all sides. And you carve off pieces of deer with your pocket knife and do your best to cook the meat, like you saw Castor do. And you're not Castor and this isn't a kitchen and you don't know the first thing about what you're doing, but you're starving hungry and the woods in winter are barren of anything that might feed you. And some is burnt and some is bloody, but you put your teeth to what's in-between and gnaw and chew, and spit at the foul taste. You force yourself to swallow it down, the skin about your mouth already stinging where the blood and juices touched it, and wait for the sickness.

Your stomach revolts in short order, but you won't let it. And perhaps its protests are more rooted in the strangeness than the true internal revolt you're expecting. You spend all night in silent argument with your innards, and every moment they let up, you go to the horrible, badly-cooked carcase and force another bite down your protesting throat. And at least it gives you something to think of beside the hunger. By morning, the snow's stopped and you gather more wood and return to the farm. And you remember. You beat the world. You did something they say people just can't do. Just as they say you can't kill an ogre.

You're just about recovered inside your head by now. The dreams don't come back often, though you'll never be wholly free of them. You can think on your father without wanting to die. You can think on Gerald without that cocktail of fear and hate and rage blanking out your mind. You have found a place with Roben's people. You're an outlaw, and that's your life. You tell yourself there are worse. Better an outlaw than a lackey of a monster like Sir Peter. Better an outlaw than a witless serf tugging your forelock as the Masters ride by in their gleaming cars.

And then you're coming back with another bundle of wood, hoping it's eggs for lunch, and there's an ogre at the Widow Neris's farm.

You drop, then you freeze. It's even odds that you might have frozen first and then stood there, out in the open, until that huge head swung round to find you.

It's not Sir Peter. This is a younger ogre, and even larger. The Widow Neris's house has two storeys, and the top of his head is level with the sill of the upper window. He wears a bulky vest and a heavy belt, both with many pockets and tools, and there's a long gun slung over his back. His hair is cropped short, but he has a savage claw of black beard jutting from his heavy chin. And he's alone, just the one ogre. No retinue of humans, no car.

Then something pads around the side of the house and you see he's not alone at all. One dog, and then a second.

You know dogs: the shepherds back home have them, and the other outlaws have often warned you that a dog is a vagabond's worst enemy, and to avoid any house that has a sign of one if you're on the scrounge. A dog, to you, is a working animal about waist high that keeps the sheep in check or barks at the unfamiliar hand on the shutter or a strange footfall outside the door.

These are something else. They come above the ogre's own waist, and to you, their heads would be level with your shoulders. Big heads, all jaw and jowl. They're muscular and sleek. Every movement speaks of the strength and speed of them. You fear those dogs like you've never feared a living thing in your life, even an ogre. Even your father when you made him really mad at you.

And you're away, firewood abandoned, scurrying low to keep off the skyline and heading for the trees. Abandoning Roben's people, but then what could you do? If they're at the farm, then the ogre has them, and if they're not, you don't know where they are anyway. Maybe they're already dead. Did you see blood about the chops of those hounds? Maybe the Widow Neris and her family lie torn apart, strewn through the rooms of their home. Because who is there to tell an ogre 'no'? Do you really believe there is justice for an ogre who kills a man, besides a harsh word and perhaps some tax or a fine? You do not.

And you know he's hunting you, and any harm he's done is on your head. And if you stopped and examined that thought, you'd realise it needn't be so. But you've no chance to stop because you're running too fast, and anyway, as matters turn out, you're right.

Somehow you'd almost forgotten what you did. The thing the ogres were never going to forgive. Of course they've been hunting you.

So you flee through the woods. You find a stream that's still more water than ice and you splash through it, because Garett once told you that's how you shake a dog that's after you. You look for trees to climb, only to abandon the notion the moment you find them. You run until you're stumbling tired and then you realise you're lost in the woods, deeper in the trees than even the outlaws go, and the dark is drawing on.

And there are worse things than deer and boar in the outlaws' tales. In the deep woods, where humans aren't likely to be met, the Masters have stocked the trees with special beasts for their special hunts. Bears, they say; wolves that are like giant dogs with teeth like blades. Or other things that belong to no kin or kind but are of themselves only, made by the sorcery of the ogres. Some of them were humans once, they say. Humans who offended the Masters with their laziness or their impudence, or just by crossing their paths at the wrong moment. Perhaps that'll be your fate. After all, what you did was much worse.

Still breathing hard, you look up and see the first dog.

It is like a shadow, a piece of the night come a little early. It pads between the trees, deceptive in its silence. Probably it had its nose to the ground all the way from the Widow Neris's place, but now its round eyes are fixed on you. It casts its snout to the canopy and howls in triumph.

You'd thought you were run out, but it turns out there's still some run left in you. Dashing between the trees, bouncing off them, tripping over roots and fallen branches, skidding through a sudden clearing where a circle of snow lies undisturbed by any tracks save yours. And the feet of the dogs behind you make no sound, but you hear their breath synced with your racing heart. You see them at the corner of your eye as they race to cut you off. And you run faster and faster, like that nightmare where all the speed in the world will not stretch the distance between you and your pursuers. In your head you're still looking for a stream to throw them off, even though they've seen you. You're still looking for a tree.

And there's a tree, and you throw yourself at the lowest branch and hook your elbows over it, fighting to haul yourself up by main strength. It's a desperate plan and it has no Part Two, but you don't even complete Part One because the lead dog has rushed forwards and its jaws close on your shin like a saw-toothed vice.

You scream, but for a moment you hang on. Then the dog puts its weight behind its jaws and the pain of your shredded flesh is too much. You come down hard and the dogs are at you, snarling, slavering, teeth clamping on your sleeves, your shoes, your hands as you bring them up to defend your face. You curl up to shelter the tender parts of you that they doubtless want to rip into. They pull you left and right with appalling force.

You're big and strong. You've always been comfortably aware of it. Perhaps that's what let you open Gerald Grimes's throat when any other human would have cowered and wept. But these dogs make a toy of you. And, at last, one of them has your arm in its bone-crushing jaws and the other has its clawed feet on your chest, barking like thunder right in your face so that your whole world resounds with it.

And this is a part of your hero's journey, like the rest. Every hero has their nadir that they must rebuild from. And you will always remember this fear, that turns your voice to a high treble of tremble and pleading, that soaks your trousers with your own urine.

Then the barking stops and your arm is released, though one dog still has its massive weight on your chest, keeping you down. Their master – their Master – has arrived.

He laughs, the ogre. His bulk slides into your view past the suspicious glower of his pets. You see his nose wrinkle.

"You stink of piss, monkey," he tells you. "Strip off."

Even then you protest, but at a signal the dogs are barking at you, both of them, right in your face, and you whimper and weep and end up naked by your own hands, freezing in the cold. And you think he'll call the dogs off then, but he sets them on you, feinting and lunging, snapping at your dangling genitals, barking and growling, until you're backed up against a tree, the bark scarring your skin, screaming for mercy at the top of your voice.

He lets the dogs rip your clothes apart in a vicious game of tug-of-war. You're given a blanket and he starts a fire with a bottle of some liquid that sets even wet wood blazing at a spark. "You run now," he tells you, "even the dumbest monkey's going to see you're not from round these parts, being butt-naked. But I don't think you'll run. You'll think of Catch and Tongs here, and you'll stay right where I put you." You learn the names of his dogs before you learn his.

He brings you back to the Widow Neris's house first of all. The Widow and her family are all still there, though terrified of what you've brought down on them. And you do feel a spark of relief, despite your fear and shame. They've not gone the way of your father; collateral damage of your temper and stupidity. There is some mercy in the world, just not for you.

The ogre eats them out of house and home. He has them kill the fattest hens and shouts at the girls about how to cook them. Half the rest of the flock go to the dogs, which he lets riot in the coop until they've had their fill of feathers and blood. He burns up their whole stock of wood to keep his feet warm at the hearth. He devours bread and cheese and mushrooms and most of the rest of the larder. You get crusts and rind, but by then you're hungry enough to eat anything.

There's no sign of Roben's people. They got out, you hope, rather than being dog-torn carcasses piled out the back of the house. Then, long after dark, there's a voice outside you know, calling in quavering tones for 'Theo'. That's how you learn the ogre's name.

He goes out with the dogs and, because he's no fool, he brings you too. He doesn't want to run the whole chase again, however much fun he had the first time.

And it's Manx Jack, of all Roben's people the one closest to you in age and temperament. He's keeping a wary distance, hopping from foot to foot, but he's been bold enough to hail the ogre from his den. For a moment you think this is some rescue, that all of Roben's people and a hundred bold outlaws more will surround the house, slay the monster and save you. But it's not that. It's something meaner and more wretched.

"You said," says Jack, "you'd find me somewhere." He's wringing his hands together like he'll never get them clean.

"If I told you, you said you... I can't take this life, sir. I can't take another year without a roof, without a place."

And Theo nods massively, staring at him. "I said that, did I?" And even then you're only just starting to understand that Jack sold you out. He heard word of an ogre on the prowl, from the girls most like, and saw the chance to escape the outlaw life he always professed to love.

"You think," Theo tells him, "there's a place in polite company for such as you?" And then the dogs are padding past him, full of murdered fowl but no less hungry for action despite that. And Manx Jack turns and flees, but the dogs are faster and, unlike you, Theo has no interest in bringing him in alive.

CHAPTER FOUR

You think Theo's going to take you home, or maybe to Sir Peter, but ogres have their ways. Theo's art and profession is the bringing in of runaways like you, and he wants to have his full credit for the catch. Which means he's taking you further from home than you've ever been.

You've heard of the train. Nothing for humans, but the ogres use it to transport goods fast over long distances. Theo takes you to the rail, a gleaming silver line that cuts through the forest, the trees carved back from it twenty feet on either side with an eerie precision. You walk alongside it for some time. He's let you have your shoes, but other than that it's the blanket and nothing beneath it, so you're shivering and numb by then, and only the fear of the dogs is keeping you going. You can't feel your feet, and you know from Roben's talk that you may lose your toes and fingers, nose, ears… But Theo doesn't care and he says he'll have Catch and Tongs drag you by your dick if you don't walk. You're going to die, he tells you. They'll execute you for the murder, and they'll make it hard and painful and record images of it to show to other monkeys who might have ideas about raising a hand against their Masters. But it still won't be as painful as being torn apart by dogs. And so you walk.

The train goes by once, and you end up hunched over on hands and knees with your hands over your ears, because it is *too* fast and *too* loud and you never imagined there was anything like it in the world. And then Theo has you at the depot, a great building of windowless grey stone, with a whole tribe of people whose lives are in receiving boxes and sacks and putting them on and off the snaking carriages of trains. They have machines, like little cars with a great claw on the front, to lift and stack the crates and pallets they move around. You've never seen humans allowed to use that kind of ogre craft before. They stare at you fearfully, as though your mere presence might mean your doom will rub off on them. There's no sympathy in their ashen, sunken faces.

Theo throws you bodily aboard the next train when it screeches to a halt. It's not a transport meant for people, you can see. A long snake of house-sized containers, and a couple of enclosed compartments where the depot tribe stack their smaller items. That's where you go, huddled in your blanket and pinned by the baleful stare of the dogs.

When the train gets up to speed you half expect to black out from the sheer noise and fury of it, but somehow inside it isn't the same. As though it's the world beyond that's been unlocked to rush away from you, and you're at the still centre of it.

Theo's looking at you. Not a mean look, perhaps even a bit of humour in it. You've not looked him in the face before, but now you dare it. Like most ogres, his monstrosity is purely in his size: your head comes about to the middle of his chest and even for one of the Masters he's massively built. He meets your timorous gaze and smiles, and you see he has tusks, just like kids always say ogres have; just like they don't have, except he does. He just loves your reaction, has been waiting for it. Much later, you get told he had them put in specially, grown there by ogre magic, purely to frighten human people.

"Been hunting monkeys a long time," he rumbles. "Not one like you, though." He sounds almost approving. For a moment you think he means the chase you led him, but he disabuses you of that in short order. "You run like shit. Thought you'd be more sport. A killer." He kicks out at you lazily. "Stand up. Lose the blanket."

You make to argue but Catch growls, deep and low, and so you're standing up and butt-naked save for your shoes before the ogre's assaying gaze. There's nothing prurient in it, just a professional taking stock, as though you were a fish that might or might not break some kind of record.

"Big enough monkey, though," he admits. "I've been after killers before. Not many, but some. A cook who poisoned his master. A nanny smothered a babe. Never knew a monkey that just up and stabbed a man to death." He stands up. "Fancy your luck with me, do you, monkey?" This is an ogre train, so he can stand up to his full height, his full breadth. "I give you my pen-knife, you'll open old Theo up and feed his guts to the dogs, will you?"

And maybe when they tell this part of your story, you'll make some dire prophecy, about how he and you will meet again, and you'll do all those things and triumph, like a hero should. But what you actually do is mumble and look away and tremble, and who would blame you? He's twice your weight and quick with it, and the dogs wouldn't just sit idly by. You and he have an understanding about exactly who has the leverage, and how little a knife would change that.

And he doesn't give you a knife anyway. Because he has to sleep some time, and maybe the dogs would stop you opening that broad throat or maybe they wouldn't. And even then, at your lowest ebb, you recognise that tacit admission of vulnerability. The strength of ogres is a grand thing, but with a good enough lever even a human can change the world, and a knife is a powerful lever, as Gerald Grimes found out.

"Did you kill the others?" you ask.

Theo's eyes widen a little. He wasn't expecting you to talk back. And if he'd killed Roben and the rest, he'd be boasting of it right then. They got away, then, and likely Manx Jack was good enough to warn them of the company he had coming round. "You didn't bring Jack in," you add. "The man your dogs killed."

"No bounty on him. But you are the golden monkey-king of fugitives. You've made me rich with your fucking knifework." He doesn't seem particularly sad that Gerald Grimes is dead, and you vaguely understand that it's not justice for Gerald that slapped that big bounty on your head. It's that you raised your hand against the Masters. The crime that got your father rendered down and served up in your stead; that you then repeated and magnified. You stepped out of your place in the world, the role the pastor always droned on about, which that hymn immortalised. *The Master in his castle, the poor man at his gate…* Your offence was not against just the ogres, it was against the ordered universe. And perhaps for some that thought would inspire dread and shame, but you're a hero and heroes are supposed to transgress, to rise above their native estate. You feel a stab of pride that you have earned a special death. Perhaps the ogres will remember you and your knife, when you're gone. Perhaps ogre children will tell each other of the murderous monkey who might come for them. Or else they'll execute you in such a grand and hideous way that your death will expunge your entire life and be the only thing anyone ever remembers about you.

You sleep a little – the train is warmer than the winter outside, at least – and then Theo kicks you awake because you've arrived.

Birchill Interchange is the place. It's somewhere several train rails converge, and there is a cluster of brutal, grey buildings there like the depot. They're built for ogres, but mostly it's just people scurrying in and out of them.

There's another whole village-worth here who do nothing but keep the wheels of the ogres' world turning. It's not just goods, either, but ideas that come here to be ordered and disposed of. An 'administrative hub,' those are the words you learn later. And one thing that gets dealt with here is justice. One of the drab, grey buildings is a jail, temporary storage for bad monkeys. Temporary because nobody's going to waste the space and resources to keep a human locked up for long. Ogre justice doesn't wait around.

Theo drops you off there. He gives you into the hands of another ogre, shorter and stouter than him – only ten inches taller than you, perhaps, but far heavier. Theo obviously gets whatever he was promised and walks away whistling, Catch and Tongs at his heels. You get thrown into a windowless grey room and locked in utter darkness. The only improvement to your circumstances is they give you clothes, bright yellow and marked with black triangles so, should you ever get out, everyone would know you instantly for the criminal you are.

The next day, Sir Peter comes to see you. And you're a long way from his estates, but of course the ogres can travel swift as the wind when they need to. That stately progressing from village to village was just him indulging himself. Probably he's had a carriage on a train to himself, or used a flying machine to skip across the world until he came to Birchill Interchange.

You've been dragged out to a bigger room. They've put metal cuffs on you, locking your wrists behind your back. Humans did all this, not the squat ogre in charge. He doesn't get his hands dirty touching monkeys, but he has a staff of hard humans, like Sir Peter's beaters. And they beat you when you won't cooperate. They write bruises all over your skin with their truncheons until you let them bind you. And you're bigger and stronger than any of them, you realise. As though living here without the sun and the open sky, right in the ogres' shadow, has shrivelled them up. But there are many of them and they hold you down and beat and kick you until, when you come bound before Sir Peter, you feel like half the execution's been done already.

Sir Peter stands over you. You wait for the rage, the frothing. You see the clenched jaw, the throbbing vein at his temple. He has his stick, his knuckles white about the head.

He beats you. We won't dwell on it. Had it been Theo, younger and more massive still, there would have been broken bones rather than just a mosaic of bruises laid across your skin, and perhaps there would have been death. Had he been mad with grief, a father for his son, then perhaps the same. But the beating Sir Peter gives you is almost clinical. He lines up each stroke and keeps his anger on a leash, like Theo's dogs never needed. A lash of agony across your arm or leg or back, and then a contemplative moment as the echo of your cry batters about the close walls of the room. And then another, where you're least expecting it, but precise. And you understand even then that he's making sure he doesn't rob the executioner.

And on the eighth blow the stick comes down across your thigh and snaps when its end strikes the hard ground, and Sir Peter stands there and you share a look, the two of you. His eyes flick from you to the broken cane and it's almost as if he's going to laugh at the absurdity of it, and expect you to join in.

He leaves then, with the air of a man satisfied for now, and you assume they'll make an end of you immediately, bruises and all. But there are ogrish wheels working behind the scenes, slow and sure, and your captivity drags out the next few days. And Sir Peter isn't the only ogre to come and see you.

Mostly it's lone men, but sometimes they bring their wives. One even has a brood of four ogre children along, monstrous chubby cherubs the size of a grown man. Unlike Sir Peter, who had honest parental grief as his grievance, they come to gawp. They come to see the human who would dare shed the blood of their own. As Theo said, you're special. And they spit at you. They sneer. They tell each other in loud voices how you'll meet a suitable fate, treacherous vermin that you are. And, although they don't mean to, they give something back to you that Theo and his dogs and the chase took away. You accomplished something they hadn't seen before when you struck back at Gerald. You cracked the foundations of their world, and behind all their jeering and laughing and spite is just a little thread of nervousness.

And in the midst of all of these comes the Baroness Isadora Lavaine.

You don't mark her much at the time, but you'll know her soon. If anything strikes you, it's that she's the only ogress who comes alone, with no chaperone or husband.

A mountain of a woman, statuesque and grand, wearing a long coat of ivory velvet and spike-heeled shoes. Sir Peter's wife never travelled with him on his taxation rounds. You've not seen much of ogre women before. Isadora: with her great tide of dark hair, the hard lines about her eyes and mouth, the sheer mass of her.

The next day, though, after the gawpers have been and gone, it's Isadora you're brought before. And not just her. There's another ogre there, a great mutton-chopped monster of a man, as wide as Sir Peter and as tall as Theo, wearing a suit of gleaming grey and a red cravat. He is, you soon understand, some sort of ogre official. There aren't many, because they tend to devolve that sort of bureaucratic chore to their human minions, but sometimes a decision is required that carries responsibility, and that is something the ogres reserve for themselves. Although not for the grand amongst them, is your impression. The suited ogre is sweating and unhappy, and it's because he has Isadora on one side and Sir Peter on the other.

You stand there with manacled hands, and the three ogres lounge behind a long desk as big as two carts laid together. They've brought you in specifically so they can discuss you as though you aren't there.

"He does seem a powerful physical specimen, for an Economic." Isadora gives the word, which you've never heard before, special emphasis. She stares at you keenly. "Can we have him stripped, warden?" At the two other ogres' looks, she smirks. "Purely in the interests of research, gentlemen. And he actually killed your son in an altercation,

Peter? Not just slit his throat when he was drunk?" Beyond the details, the fact of Gerald's death seems to matter not at all to her.

Sir Peter stands abruptly, face purpling with rage as it never did when he was beating you. For a moment he chokes around a response, and then Isadora actually laughs politely.

"Well, then," she says. "I simply must have him."

"That is… irregular," says the warden awkwardly.

"Nonetheless. You know I have the authority." And then she says, "*Droit de science*," which you don't understand then, but will in time.

"I protest," Sir Peter gets out. "We must make an example of him." He makes aborted gestures at you, trying to find the words for something so obvious it shouldn't need saying. "For the other monkeys."

"Well exactly," Isadora drawls, her eyes still roving over you. "And don't you think we need to find out why our golden boy here has done what the Economics" – that word again – "aren't supposed to. Quite the aberration. I need blood samples, psych evaluations, all the fun of the fair. I am, gentlemen, *intrigued*." Her voice is light and full of whimsy right up until the point it collapses to a steel edge. "And when I am *intrigued,* I get what I want."

"No," Sir Peter spits out, as the warden vacillates.

"Why, Peter, it's almost as though you're desperate to repay your father's debts," she says sweetly, and he goes such an unnatural, angry colour you think he might die there and then, but instead he just storms away, leaving her with the warden and the field.

"Have him gift-wrapped," she says, "and sent to my VTOL." *Vee-toll*, you hear, and don't understand. "I'll take full responsibility."

And that is that, your fate decided.

BY THAT EVENING you're at her estate, from one windowless cell to another. You'd thought the train was serious ogre magic, but she carried you to her home in a flying machine that screamed all the way and left your head ringing with its agonised voice. You lay on the floor of its belly, and Isadora sat there with ear guards on. And so did the three humans, one man and two women, that were her attendants, while another controlled the machine.

Three more days you're in that cell, manacled save when you eat or void your bowels. The lights are always on, though you're so tired and hopeless that you still sleep most of the time. They daub the dog bites with stinging potions. They come and needle out tubes of your blood, snip swatches of hair, scratch at the inside of your cheeks. You think it's punishment at first. The people who inflict this on you are neat, white-clad. They talk to each other in brisk, efficient voices using words you don't know, and treat you like a thing. And you think of livestock back on the farm, and how sometimes they were sick. The old women and men who knew about such things would take samples of their dung and their piss, look into their eyes and at their tongues. So that's what they're doing with you. Finding out what's wrong with you. Not for a cure, but so they can make sure the same defect doesn't happen in other people.

And then they come for you, on the fourth day, and their manner is different. No needles, no swabs, no little containers for your bodily fluids.

"Dress," says one of them. "The Mistress wishes to see you." The clothes are white, like theirs, tight across the shoulders and short at the cuffs. And if you'd been your old bullish self, perhaps you'd have scattered the three attendants like ninepins and gone bowling around Isadora's home, battering at the windows for a way out like a demented fly. Poor food and Sir Peter's stick have done sufficient damage that you dress meekly before their clinical gaze. And then they lead you out and up some stairs, and you're in a grand house where the midday sun streams in through the windows to blanche the geometries of the art on the far wall. And the light brings something back to you that was missing since the dogs had you in their teeth, so that, when the attendants bring you to Isadora's presence, there's a bit of the hero returned to you, stepping into the monster's lair.

And it's a great hall, one wall a vast window looking out on a tangle of other buildings, squat and unlovely like Birchill Interchange had been. One thing you'll learn about Isadora is that she doesn't care much for the sculpted parks and grounds of other ogres. Her estate is designed to *do* things, rather than just act as a multi-acre demonstration of conspicuous consumption.

She sits at the big table at one end of the hall, beneath a

bizarre picture that you'll spend a long time staring at, on and off over the coming years. At first you think it's surely drawn by a child. There are lines crossing other lines, people drawn with eyes both on the same side of their face. There's a cow in the same style, and at first you almost laugh at it. And then you don't laugh, and a strange, cold feeling comes to you, staring up at it. Because it's a terrible thing. A record of a terrible thing. There is agony and grief in the lines of those strange, misproportioned figures. You want to shy away from it and yet your eyes won't leave it alone. Eventually their only possible refuge is in looking at Isadora herself.

She beckons, and you walk down the length of the room, around the long low table where a score of humans are sitting and eating – in the same room as their betters, no less! They are all wearing the same white uniform. Some wear spectacles, which you saw on an ogre once but never on a human. They are mostly women, just a handful of men amongst them. They watch you curiously, taking in your rough strength that no more belongs here than a bull from your home pastures would.

The Baroness Isadora Lavaine leans forwards on her elbows to look down on you. Tower over the menials as much as you like, she'd still be head and shoulders taller if she stood, and over a hundred pounds heavier. Her vast wealth of gleaming dark hair is coiled up atop her head, secured with long pins and adding another six inches to her height.

You stand there like a dumb thing, mouth open, eyes dancing from her to the picture to the servants' table.

"Welcome, Torquell," Isadora tells you. She has a sly, measuring smile you'll become more than familiar with, from the many, many times in life that she gets her own way. Over you, over other ogres, over the world. Better that than the sour look her face lapses into otherwise, because of all of her kind, Isadora is not content with the ways of the world, and she'll trample over every institution and rule to change it.

"Is this a trick?" It's all you can think of to say. You look so lost. All your life in the vicinity of a single peasant village under the rule of Sir Peter Grimes, who cares only that his peons contribute to his perfect little agricultural yesteryear, and now this.

"False hope before the execution?" She laughs, like genial thunder. "Bit much, just for you, don't you think? No, dear, that's off." Pronounced with an exaggerated emphasis. *Orff*. "I've got more than enough clout to overrule Peter fucking Grimes any day of the week."

And you stammer out a question that would be impudence enough to have you whipped, back where you come from. You ask who she is.

Isadora grins and singles out a young woman sitting at the head of her staff table. This worthy stands up smartly and announces, "The Baroness Isadora Trenchent Lavaine, Doctor of Natural and Unnatural Philosophy." It's a joke between ogres, you understand later. Or at least a joke at the other ogres' expense. Isadora doesn't rate her fellow Masters highly.

"And you, young Torquell, are an intriguing little

monster," Isadora of the grand titles informs you. "And so I have decided to snatch you from the jaws of death and keep you around. Welcome to my staff."

CHAPTER FIVE

AND THE SUGGESTION of ownership perhaps engenders a little jolt of opposition in you. If you'd been the lad you were before Sir Peter's visit – so full of yourself and full of mischief – then maybe you'd have said something unwise to Isadora's face. But that was before Gerald; that was before Theo and the dogs. Right now, you've had something of that lad beaten out of you by fate and the ogres, and you just take it, to all outward show. But inside you, something still sparks rebellion, as later events will demonstrate.

But for now, and for years to come, you're of Isadora's household. Because you've got nowhere else, no going home for you. Because it's better than standing naked before the hounds, covering your shrivelled manhood and shivering in the winter air.

You take your place at table and eat unfamiliar food. The others make room for you, cast sideways looks. This isn't a band of roistering youths from the village whom you'll naturally rise to lead. They aren't like any people you ever met before. Isadora has precise requirements as to who she'll accept on her staff. Requirements that, you soon work out, should exclude you entirely.

You have your letters; your father was insistent on it, and despite a history of truancy and malingering you were actually a sharp enough student. The pastor and the schoolmistress were able to give you reading and writing and maths by dint of patience and cursing and words with your father when your focus slackened. But the white-coated women and men – and you work out very quickly it's the women who come first in Isadora's retinue – have an education beyond anything you ever dreamt of. They understand magic.

The first thing they understand about it is that there's no such thing as magic. They have other words for the marvels of the ogre world. Moreover, they understand how to make those marvels, are actively engaged in finding more marvels yet; all under Isadora's guidance, the Mistress of all that is marvellous.

They do not approve of you. They are entirely polite, but you are not of their order or sorority. They were all hand-picked for both the quickness of their minds and their industry in putting those minds to use. The former is something you can probably lay claim to, the latter not so much. Things always came easily to you, and so you never really worked at them. You never had that soaring ambition to take the world apart to see how it worked. And nobody is slowing their headlong rush so that you might catch up. You're welcome to learn, seems to be the ground rule, but Isadora's interest in you isn't because you're a monkey genius.

Chief amongst the staff, and your personal nemesis, is a young woman named Minith. She is small, neat, her dark hair cut short as with most of the staff. She is Isadora's lieutenant of marvels. You hear the other staff bring questions to her, but you never hear one she has no answer for, even if that answer is simply a suggestion about what to look for or how to investigate. Your own questions, that you are full of, go untended. The few you do try, early on, meet with utter contempt, as though you'd gone to a shepherd and cluelessly speculated as to where lambs come from. After that, you are so wounded by the reception that you mostly stop asking. Left to your own devices, you'd avoid Minith entirely, and away from her presence perhaps lure one or two of the others into some tentative friendship. She seems ubiquitous, however, supervising, spying on you, reporting to her Mistress. Or fetching you and bringing you to Isadora in the grand library, when the Mistress wants to see you. Which is often. She has many questions for you, as though she's going to compile some kind of history of your brief life and your longer genealogy. She has Minith stay and record your talk, both on devices that can speak your voice back to you, and with words written on paper. Minith plainly feels all this is beneath her, most especially that she is having to have her life orbit yours even for a moment. When she takes you out of the library, her glare suggests you are an insect, a pest she'd rather eradicate from the estate and grounds. And, because Minith feels that way, the rest of the staff avoid you. From being the centre of your village's social scene you have become a hermit. The only person you actually share many words with, in those early days and weeks and months, is Isadora herself. She is fascinated by you.

That, you guess, is what really riles Minith. That you are monopolising her precious Mistress's time.

Two months of this – of you kicking your heels in the corridors of Hypatian, the name Isadora has given to her grand house; of staring at the strange art that doesn't look like anything in the real world and yet somehow still fish-hooks emotions out of you; of getting the cold shoulder from the staff; of Isadora's sending for you every few days. Two months, and then you finally come to the crux because she asks you about the day Sir Peter came.

You tell the story, and find that you can. Your voice doesn't shake. Your father's death and that of Gerald Grimes are both told in the same flat voice. You even meet her gaze, look straight into her eyes as you say the words. You are determined not to give her the slightest window onto your grief, and enough time has passed since the deaths and the dogs that you are master of yourself.

"Hmm…" She eyes you speculatively, and then Minith moves forwards and attaches things to you – to your wrists, your temples, your bared chest, clinical and brisk. Clear rubber discs linked by wires to another machine.

"Tell me again." Isadora leans forwards, a few locks of her dark hair slithering out of place. Her tongue moistens her lips. "Tell me about when you came home, and what you found."

You tell her, and she questions you, and you tell her again. Her words stalk remorselessly about the barriers of your resolve until they find a crack, and then they work their way in like roots. The ice boxes; the bones; the realisation that you'd brought it on yourself. Gerald's mocking glee. Minith's pen records everything, as do the machines in their separate ways. And at last you stumble over the bland narrative, the retellings not coating the memory in a protective layer of shell as you intended, but rasping rough-tongued until it's all raw and exposed again. Until you feel the anger you felt then, at yourself, at the world, at the *Masters*. At *how dare they*. At the order of the world that let such things happen.

"Good," says Isadora, though you cannot see anything that is *good* about either what happened then or what is happening now. She is consulting something in a mirror on her desk. "Excellent. Torquell, you've been a darling boy."

And that's almost it. She's an ogress, after all, and you're no more than a monkey to her. Or an 'Economic' as she puts it. But something shifts in her face, then, as she looks on yours.

"I won't ask you to go through this again, Torquell," she says. "That's done with. I have what I need." It's not much, as sympathy goes. It's not hugs and consolation; it's certainly not an apology. But you have been an exile in this company for two months, and an orphan and a fugitive before that, and sometimes it only takes the slightest kindness.

You are crying before you realise, and you have enough self-possession to hate yourself for it, but some streams just can't be dammed. And she watches, and there's a certain amount of academic interest on her face – the machines are still recording, after all – but you see a little empathy, too. Uncomfortable, writ into the lines of her outsized perfection, but there nonetheless. And then she has Minith take you to go get supper, and Minith, of course, loathes every moment with you. Hates it that you have taken even a sliver of her Mistress's love, that which might otherwise have gone to Minith herself.

A while after that, you are fitted for some new clothes. Not just a fresh suit of white that actually fits your heftier build, given that even the biggest of the staff is still several inches shorter and narrower, but a coat of green velvet with mustard britches, stockings, buckled shoes, shirts. Your hair is cut short and you get the smoothest shave you ever had in your life.

"She's taking you to a party," Minith tells you. By then, you've had enough of her, and the new clothes are a kind of armour against her scorn.

"Instead of you, you mean."

For a moment she just stares. It's the first time you've risen to the bait.

"Oh, I'll be there. Her Ladyship takes me everywhere." Not quite the brag you were expecting, just a statement of fact. Minith's face is closed and unreadable. "She'll have you standing behind her chair, waiting on her. You can do that, can you? And not disgrace us?"

You're aware of the practice, that the Masters must have their attendants for every little thing. You shrug. "We'll find out."

IT'S NO GRAND affair, this first time. Lady Isadora does end up at the great ogre gatherings, but her work is more important to her; she puts in an appearance only when there's advantage in it for her. So you learn later. Right now, this is as grand a function as you're ready for. A ride in the screaming *vee-tol*, landing on the roof of a great mansion, a room full of nightmarish animals stuffed into glass cases; five other ogres, vast and overdressed and unsparing of the wine. Isadora holding court.

She is magnificent. The thought surprises you. She is the only ogress, the rest are all men. They are all learned, magicians of the sciences that she practices. And you know by then that a great estate run by one unmarried ogress is strange, as is a staff that is almost all human women. Isadora is an eccentric, and by all rights she should be an outcast and a recluse. Except she plays the room like a musical instrument: flirts, teases, scorns advances, shouts over them when she needs to; dominates the conversation. And you understand very little of it, all that talk of base pairs and genetics and some manner of 'inheritance' which is plainly little to do with who gets which cow after the funeral. And eventually enough wine has sloshed about the room that they're mostly into anecdotes.

They are what your home village would have called sorcerers. Not in the way most ogres are, with all their machines and devices, but the real thing, the ogres who know the secrets of the universe and how to unlock them. You hear a vast barrel of a man with a beard like a thornbush roar with laughter as he describes the new birds he's bred that hunt better than any hound. ("Retrieved from extinction!" he cackles. "Dinosaurs next!" And the words mean nothing, not yet.) Another is talking machines and mechanics of some sort, a third speaks of pathways that are somehow inside the body and can be manipulated to conjure pleasure and pain. A fourth loves only insects and speaks of raising and quelling plagues, of places you never heard of stripped bare in the name of scientific enquiry. "All got a bit out of hand," he smirks, and they snicker along with him. Isadora – as drunk as the rest and yet still Mistress of what's said and who gets to say it – derides some, woos others, and laughs as vastly as the rest, head flung back so that her merriment echoes from the rafters.

"Is this," asks an old man, "the one you wrote to me about?" He's looking at you.

You don't look back. That is a thing you do not do with ogres. You did with Isadora, and somehow that didn't get you whipped or beaten, but you know enough not to try it with this one. He's the mechanics man, a mind of metal and wheels.

"None other." Isadora leans back and regards you fondly.

At her beckon, you come unwillingly forwards into the massed pressure of their gaze.

"Robust little monkey, ain't he?" one of them remarks.

"An atavism, you say?" Mechanics-mind isn't convinced. "You didn't breed the fellow up on one of your test farms?"

"Why would you?" one of the others demands. "Who has any use for turning monkeys into gorillas?"

"The generals are always lamenting the quality of their troops," says the insect-master with a superior sneer, and there's much braying and snorting over that. Whoever the generals are, these educated men don't rate them much.

"Stuyfer would thrash him," says Mechanics-mind. "My man, Stuyfer. I'll lay a hundred pounds on it."

Stuyfer is brought forwards. He's a big, broad man, which is to say he's as broad as you but not as tall. He wears a dark coat, and he has a metal hand. He takes the coat off slowly – mechanically, you might say – and the whole arm is metal, sheathed in a plastic skin that is transparent precisely so you can see the workings. The skin where it joins his torso is scarred and angry. Mechanics-mind is explaining how Stuyfer lost the limb in the mills, providing an opportunity for the ogre scientist to experiment. Stuyfer's flat face is expressionless as his history and mutilation is discussed.

"What do you think, Torquell?" Isadora asks you. "Do you think you can take him?" Her face is flushed with drink, but there is a sly look there, not as abandoned as she is pretending for the benefit of her peers. And they're a little incredulous she's even asking you, and it's a curious shared moment, when it's you and her. You find that, before that braying crowd of other ogres, you want to make her proud of you. You nod.

They go into the next room and shove all the furniture to the walls, not even calling for servants to do it. The ogres sit around the edges and you and Stuyfer face off.

The fight is curious. You take several blows from his flesh and bone left hand, including one solid strike to the eye that almost floors you. You don't let that metal fist land, though, and Stuyfer never seems to understand that he could use your reticence to control the fight and dictate where you go. You've been in scraps plenty of times as a youth, and you're used to taking it and dishing it out. Stuyfer doesn't react when you hit him, not face, not gut. A kick between the legs that has the ogre lords wincing barely yields a reaction. The man is like a machine in more ways than one, and you're tiring and he's not. He's not quick, but he just slogs on like cogs and gears. Right then, it makes him monstrous, implacable, and you know you've made a mistake and sooner or later the steel fist will find a bone to break, a skull to crack.

Later, after you've learned, you realise the man must have been up to his eyeballs in painkillers and other medication, barely present in his own head, but right now his sheer lack of responsiveness makes him a terror to you.

The next time he lashes out at you, you feel the wind of it across your face and he smashes a hole in the wall, through panelling and plaster and denting to the stone. A shock of fear takes you, as you understand he'll kill you if he hits you. Even if he doesn't intend to, he'll kill you.

So you do the mad thing, the reckless thing, just as you've always ended up doing in your life. You close and grapple. You take that mechanical arm and you put all your strength to it, bending it against where it joins the living parts of Stuyfer. You twist until you feel parts of him give, as he slams you with elbow and knee and yanks at your hair. And in the end, your living limbs are stronger—not stronger than his metal one, but stronger than where flesh and steel meet—and you are left with the arm as trophy, and Stuyfer is on the ground. He screams now, and it's almost a relief; you feel it must even be a relief to *him*, to have an outlet for his pain.

"So much for your tuppenny Grendel, my lord," Isadora crows. "A hundred pounds, wasn't it?" And then, turning to you and looking at the many bruises already flowering across your face. "Get yourself to the kitchen. Tell Minith she's to patch you up. Tell her that's my order." Because she's well aware Minith has no love for you.

Minith is eating in the kitchen, with a couple of Isadora's other staff and a handful of the locals. She looks you over and scowls when you tell her what's required, but she goes to fetch the first-aid box anyway, giving you pills and painting restorative on your bruises.

"Can't have you looking ugly for Her Ladyship," she mutters. "You've learned a new trick, then? Learned to dance? Does beating another human make you feel useful?"

And you've had a rough evening, what with the machine-man trying to kill you, and you snap and grab her arm, a hard pincer that'll leave bruises of its own, and you ask her,

"What is it? What have I done that you hate me so?"

She stares at you, frozen by the presumption of the contact. "Hate," she says, "is a strong word."

"Contempt, then."

"Yes, that's fair." No attempt to wrench herself free, staring at you, close enough to bite you on the nose and looking as though she's considering it. "You're a waste, Torquell. You've been saved from a peasant's life and a criminal's death. You've been given pride of place in a house of learning, a place that is unique, as far as I know, in any of the Masters' domains. And why?"

"I don't know."

"No, you don't. And you've never even asked. You've never *tried* to find out. You know what we do, in Her Ladyship's retinue? We ask questions. Questions about the universe and how it works. We don't just sit and listen to the pastor tell us it's God's plan. We *ask*. And if we found God we'd ask *Him* too. The big questions, that you've never even thought of. Why is the world the way it is? And how can we change it in the ways we want? But you? You've never asked those questions. You don't even ask the small questions, Torquell. You've not even asked why *you*. What's so special about you, that Her Ladyship lavishes so much time on you? The question that stands between your life and the gallows, and you haven't even thought to *ask* it."

You let her go. Her words have shaken you more than any blow that Stuyfer landed. "Do you know?" you ask.

Her expression is pitying. "Of course I know. I'm Her Ladyship's chief research assistant. She relies on me.

There's precious little of her work and interests that I don't understand as fully as she does." A sneer. "But it's not for me to tell. And you'll never know because you don't know enough to even work out what questions to ask."

But her haughty tone has faded a little by the end, because she can see you're not angry or dismissive. You're not the arrogant brute she took you for when you were dropped all unearned into your place of prominence in her household. When she's finished tending to your bruises, you sit in the kitchen, munching a crust and thinking. And making plans.

AFTER THAT, WHEN not actually attending Isadora, you change how you spend your time.

And Her Ladyship does have you attend on her a lot. Most days, you're called to her at some point or other, just to serve. She likes you. You're a well-turned-out monkey, and you're closer to ogre size than any of the others. She has you fetch and carry, and she makes you run and lift. She borrows some servants from other ogres and has them teach you tricks: dancing, wrestling, boxing. You excel each time, especially in any task where a burst of sudden adrenaline gives you an edge. She makes notes and takes blood samples.

And when not called on, you read. There is a library, after all. Isadora has uncounted books. Most of them are impenetrable at first, but you badger the other staff and you roam the shelves until you find simple primers, bootstrapping your own ability to read, finding books full of words pinned down and anatomised until the layers of their meanings are pulled back. And pictures. You appreciate the pictures above all. At first it's hard, because your life so far has been one you could just charm and grin your way through, and books don't respond to that. But everything changed with Gerald and Sir Peter, and now you appreciate just what abyss lies beneath you, and you work. Perhaps even Minith is forced to admit that you really do apply yourself.

And Isadora takes you with her whenever she leaves the house, just as she does Minith. You're always being trotted out to show to other ogres, and you see what Minith meant. There is a *something* to learn about you. It's not just that you are a well-proportioned monkey, a handsome pet. And sometimes you have to fight other prize human servants, but by then your almost ogrish strength is enhanced by the trainers Isadora's found, and you always win. She wins money by the fistful and mocks the men whose champions you lay low in her name, and none of it matters. The numbers that change hands are not meaningful resources but just a means of keeping score. Once, she even wins a village, an entire stretch of land, fields, people, homes. All you can think is that surely Isadora is a kinder master than the red-faced sputtering ogre she took it from. You've spoken to the servants of many other masters by then, in this house's kitchen or that manor's back rooms. You've seen men who've been whipped, women with great bruises across their face the size of an ogre's hand, children who've been caned into docility and silence. Isadora's staff, selected for their minds, with you as the prominent exception, have privileges and freedoms the others would barely even dream of. You're starting to appreciate just how lucky you are.

And then you find a book which finally teaches you the right questions.

Not the obvious questions. Not the *why me?* question. You've had that on the tip of your tongue a few times, when Isadora's seemed receptive, but you've sensed that just blundering straight into it isn't the way. Instead, you have found *one* of the big questions. Minith would be proud of you.

You wait until Isadora is in an expansive mood, by which you mean she's already put away a bottle of wine. One evening, just the two of you, and she's talking about something to do with agriculture. You thought you knew farming, coming as you do from a village where every part of life revolves around the care and maintenance of field and flock. Isadora's farming is something beyond your comprehension, talking of pest control and modified strains and all manner of things. But she loves to talk and she doesn't really care how much you follow. Talking, you suspect, is how she unlocks her mind and circumnavigates barriers to her research. You're just a convenient sounding board.

And then, when she's finished her current tirade and has you over to pour another glass, you pluck up the courage to ask.

"Your Ladyship…"

"Isadora," she tells you. You, Minith, a couple of others

are extended that theoretical privilege, though it's hard to force yourself to take her up on it. She's smiling at you fondly, though, the rosy glow of the wine warming her cheeks.

You teeter on the edge, knowing this will take you into uncharted wilds. You're very *aware* of her, the mass of her, the abundance. Her interest that, though mostly academic, takes a distinct pleasure in putting you through your paces when exercising or wrestling. You've heard stories from other households about the depredations of ogre masters, certainly. Thus far, Isadora has been content to just watch. But you are about to renegotiate your relationship, to make her re-evaluate you.

"I found a book," you say, like a confession. "There were pictures. Photographs," pronouncing the word carefully, "from a long time ago. Photographs of cities." Like the drab grey buildings of the Interchange but multiplied a thousand fold, off to all sides and up to the skies. "There were crowds of people there." Thousands of them, thronging the streets. In some photos, they were rioting, burning cars. In others they were protesting, holding placards, making demands. But so many. People beyond your dreams or nightmares. A vast field of people. And they were *people:* no ogres rose head and shoulders over them to take more than their fair space in that crowd. And you explain what you have seen and then throw yourself over the precipice and say, "I want to know how it could have been like that then; how it's like this now."

She laughs. It's not what you expected. She laughs and

sits you down beside her on the couch, a shocking breach of etiquette, but then, the wine has been flowing.

"My inquisitive little monkey." She tousles your hair. "It's been a long time. I was beginning to think you'd not a curious thought in your head. Have you asked Minith this, and she refused? She's jealous of her learning, that one. Sharp as a pin, but not good at sharing."

You haven't, but only because you know full well Minith would give you nothing for free. Isadora sees the look on your face and laughs again.

"Those pictures were from when the world was in a very bad way, Torquell. The Brink, is what they called it, afterwards. The world was… well, a lot of it was poisoned, and there were far too many people, all of them eating and breeding and just… using up everything. And there wasn't enough of everything. And it was only going to get worse. Something had to be done. We saved the world. Or our ancestors did, and now – peace and plenty." She sounds a little dismissive of the idea, nose wrinkling at the thought. "So much peace and plenty that it's hard to find an enquiring mind, and I don't just mean amongst the Economics. My peers, Torquell, are a waste of their genetic heritage. And I'd thought you were, too, but here you are asking questions." She pats your head. "Good boy."

"How was the world saved?"

She's still feeling indulgent, apparently. "People were eating too much, basically. Too many people, too many healthy appetites. And meat farming was monstrously inefficient. You must know how far livestock need to roam compared with a field of soy with the same yield." And you don't know, but there are books in the library that will tell you. "And my ancestors solved the problem and saved the world. I really mean that. My forerunners, those of my discipline. The engineers of the human genome. Because in the end, changing the world was too complicated, and left to their own devices people wouldn't change their habits, and so we had to change the people. Ever had a steak, Torquell?"

A memory of the dead deer in the forest comes to you and you flinch guiltily, shaking your head.

"There was a suite of genetic changes to make people into more efficient consumers. It was a bitter time, Torquell. Things were done… But it was in a good cause. Look at the plenty we have now."

"Changes…?"

"Turning a gene off here, turning one back on there. You'd be surprised how few modifications you have to make, and how easily you can engineer a microorganism to write those changes into the population. Changes to reduce the consumption footprint of an individual. Stop them being able to digest meat, that's a huge change. Oh, the cattle industry kicked, but so much land could be repurposed when the demand was gone, such an impact in and of itself. And science didn't stop there. I mean, there were so many things about people that were broken…"

Hurrying over the words before you can stop yourself, you blurt out. "There were no Masters, in those pictures. Everyone was the same."

Another smile, this one tugging teasingly around the edges of Isadora's mouth. "You think so, do you? Why do you think that is? Go on, Torquell, impress me."

"You... After they'd finished changing people to save the world, they used their powers to make you, the Masters?" You imagine those long-ago sorcerer-scientists, flushed with the fruits of their success, creating something greater than themselves, then being superseded by it. But you can see from her expression that you're not quite right. Isadora reclines back, regarding you slyly.

"Well, I didn't bring you here for your mind," she murmurs, and then, seeing you flush with shame, "but it appears you have one anyway. Perhaps you can be useful as more than a test subject. You can read. You have access to the books. I'll instruct Mirith to help you find volumes appropriate to your capabilities. Let's call this the first test of your brain, as opposed to just your fists and sinews. You find out the answer, about how we 'ogres' rose to rule the world, and then come back and tell me."

CHAPTER SIX

So begins your education.

The extreme reluctance with which Minith helps you is almost comical. Every time, she undertakes to demonstrate by expression, tone, and body language that she has a great many more important things to be getting on with. She is, after all, Isadora's chief assistant. The entire rest of the staff dances to her tune. But as it is her Mistress's wish, she does help you.

You discover soon enough that there aren't enough years in a human life for you to catch up with the science. You struggle through books intended for young students, and while Minith swears that the keys to the universe are concealed within, your fingers are too clumsy to fit them to the lock.

"The Brink," you tell her. "That's what I need to learn about."

She's startled. You've bearded her in the kitchens, the rest of the staff sitting down to breakfast. You're both keeping your voices low through some implicit agreement that what you're about shouldn't be the gossip of the house.

"Not these amino-acids and base-pairs and pee-aytch." You're frustrated with your own limitations, hulking over her without meaning to, though she doesn't even deign to move back. "People. I want to learn about people and what they did. Real things."

Her contempt is back again, but this time you weather it. You know, in your own way, that you're right. It's not the actual technicalities of the science that matter, for you. It's the decisions that led to them. You're all about the big picture, and you've become aware that there is a very big picture indeed, buried in the history of the world, and everything in your life seems to have been thrown up to hide it.

"Histories," Minith says, as though it's a dirty word. "Apparently we have recruited a *humanities* student."

You continue to weather her passive aggression, and to keep a rein on your own more active kind. "And?"

The *and* manifests as a stack of books beside your bed that evening, and you resume your research. They're still dry and difficult and full of words you have to look up. Full of pictures of men and women in odd clothes. Of those close-packed buildings, and sometimes those vast crowds. And it's complicated because at the time nobody called it the Brink, of course. It was just *then*, to them. Just the way the world was. And it was bad, no doubt. People were starving, in various parts of the world. People had no clean water. An overabundance of humanity, and no ogres at all. Based on these histories, easy enough for Isadora or Minith to argue that the world now is so much better. Peace, as Her Ladyship said, and plenty.

It will be a long process, your pursuit of truth, but you are to be on Isadora's staff for over six years, and despite Minith's early opinion of you, you have a sharp mind and work hard. You will never master the science, but over the months your reading improves so that you need to look up strange words less and less. You plumb the pages of ever denser and more complex volumes to track down your quarry.

You have other duties, of course, because while Isadora far prefers to be closeted with her own work, the social demands of being an ogress still clutch at her. And none of the Masters would travel without staff to take care of their needs, and she always brings you with her, as her closest attendant. As a pet, you are aware. A performing monkey. And yet she is fond of you. When you attend her, some evenings, she invites you to talk about what you've learned. You speculate about what happened, and she smiles and shakes her head and encourages you to continue with your books.

Books are what prompts one memorable trip, in fact, when you've been in her service for a year or so. Isadora has a need for certain volumes held in the collection of another ogre, and furthermore she requires some new books created.

Volumes lost to time, she tells you, but retained in electronic copy. And while she could read them on a screen, a method that you no longer think of as ogre sorcery, she prefers physical books. And, being the Baroness Isadora Lavaine, she is in a position to have them printed at her order.

You travel to a city by train. She has her own private carriage, and you believe she has chosen this manner of approach specifically to watch your reaction. Because it is a city like those in the books you've been reading. There are tall buildings, five, six storeys high, lining one side of the tracks. You see high chain-link fences with metal thorns on top, and narrow streets, and beyond them the chimneys of the factories and power stations. And people. Hundreds, thousands of people, all crammed into those buildings. There are women and children staring out dully at the train as it passes. Laundry hangs from great heavy strings overhead. In every window you see a woman at work: peeling, scrubbing, preparing food, darning. The men, Minith tells you, are in the factories. Or else they starve, because this is what she calls a 'company town,' and if you don't work then the company won't sell you company food in exchange for the company money they pay you for your toil. It is one of the ogres who owns the company, and its food and money and factories that Isadora is going to see.

There is the usual soiree, where a score of ogres gather together in a vast room and drink and talk. And there is a feast, an ogre's feast. You are behind Isadora's chair as usual, enduring the remarks of the other ogres about your unusually robust physique. There are some ogresses there who even eye you in a predatory fashion. Thus far, at least, Isadora has not commanded you to her bed, or even tried to seduce you – as though an ogress would need to. The possibility has been in your mind more than once, though, and you're not sure what you would feel about it, should things tilt that way.

And then the main course comes out, after seemingly endless confections of fish and pastry and meat, and it's defaulters' pie, whatever that is. A vast tableau of crust with bubbling gravy and meat underneath, and the ogres tucking in greedily and complaining that one end of the table or other is hogging the best pieces. And you do not understand and just stand there like a good servant, even though you see some of the other humans there – the Economics, as Isadora calls you – blanch. And only later does Minith cruelly explain that this is the last refuge of families with no work, or who fall foul of debts, or who cannot afford medicine, or have some other burden that regular wages will not lift. That, worst comes to worst, there is always something a human can sell, that an ogre can make use of. And Isadora eats with the same gusto as the rest and you remember that.

On the train back, staring out at those grey houses and the grey people who live crammed up in them, you have questions. And Isadora's happy to indulge you. Minith sits across the carriage, eavesdropping and doubtless resenting every moment her Mistress spends with you.

"Why all this?" you ask, gesturing out at the city with its sharp fences and close-packed windows. "There is so much land outside. There's food. The whole point of the Brink was that there would be more land and more food. Why do they have to live like this?" And more, the words tumbling out into an abyss with that dreadful defaulters' pie waiting at the bottom. "Why debts and wages and… things being expensive so people can't afford them, when science can make so much?"

Isadora's smile tells you it's a good question. "There's a theory held by the worthies who run the company – glorified boys' club that it is. They say that their workforce must be kept in such artificially straitened circumstances, with shortages and competition, or they wouldn't work. If you let the Economics be comfortable and happy and free of fear and want, then what if they just sat at home and did nothing? They say that unless you force people into a position where they must work or starve, no work would get done."

You think on that, and on what you've learned so far about Isadora's discipline and its foundations. "Have they proved this theory?"

Isadora raises an eyebrow.

"That's what you do with a theory, isn't it?" you press. You feel as though you're about to say something stupid at any moment, but the idea is so obvious. "Have they tried feeding and making people happy to see if they still did the work?"

Isadora laughed, and at first you think you have been stupid, but she's laughing at her peers, whom she plainly doesn't think much of. "You know," she says, between guffaws, "I don't think they ever tried. Funny, that."

* * *

BACK AT HYPATION you throw yourself back into your reading, and you remember the pie and the gusto, and there's a particular goad at your back, now, driving you on. It's an old thought, one that you can't imagine your father or the pastor or any of them, back in that insignificant little village, ever harbouring. It's watching Sir Peter arrive in his motorcade to receive the goods and tithes he never worked for, and everyone treating the visit as though it's such an honour. It's sitting in church hearing how God ordered the world to place a few on high with everyone else becoming the doting and obedient subjects of their benevolence, and being asked to agree that it was right. It's Gerald Grimes taunting you, and Theo the hound-master hunting you through the woods, not only because he's stronger and has the dogs, but because the world is designed to make him so. Who made the ogres, and how did they become lords of all creation? Because you read those histories of the Brink times, and all humans are standing shoulder to shoulder, and none in a monstrous shadow.

Injustice is what moves you. Injustice, that you were born to serve and scrape and, at the worst, go into a pie, and the ogres were born to rule and to gorge. And Minith keeps bringing the books with a sneer, safe in her position as Isadora's majordomo. No pie for her, after all, so why should she care?

And you find one book, written in a painfully dry and clinical style, talking of protests and riots, at the changes being mandated by what they call governments and corporate boards. People complaining at having their children changed, even though the world was at stake. In the book, it's cast as selfish and wasteful that anyone should resist such patently necessary measures. It was written post-Brink, after all, when these things had been accomplished and it only remained to justify them.

It was voluntary at first, you read. Those who signed up for the Economic Measures and allowed themselves and their genetic line to be modified were rewarded. They received some additional benefits from those who ruled. Later, they were stripped of whatever benefits they had unless they gave their consent. And the writer of the book applauds everyone who took that selfless step, to make their offspring into less wasteful, less angry, less space-consuming creatures. For the solution to being on the Brink was a whole suite of alterations. You already know that enquiring scientific minds like Isadora's can't leave well enough alone, and there's always something else to fix. So the old world turned and there was a new generation of perfect children who couldn't stomach meat, who were slower to anger and slower to argue. Happy people, the book insists. People without so much waste, without all that needless consumption. A race of people the world could support more readily. And from here on you'll understand, when Isadora says 'Economics.'

And in the end it came down to force and laws, and camps for those who hadn't consented to be part of the programme. With regret, the book insists. With care, with love. Camps, mandatory alteration, prisons. All with the best will in the world. All over the world. Because it was unthinkable that, others having made the necessary sacrifice, the selfish could live on unaltered. That, the book insists, would be unjust.

There is no mention of ogres. And you are picturing some rogue laboratory, some maverick scientist – whom you imagine with Isadora's face – deciding that they can make other improvements to the next generation; siring a brood of huge, dominating monsters with a taste for human flesh; unleashing them on an unsuspecting world that could not resist them.

You visit villages much like your own. Isadora, like most ogres, owns land, though she has lesser ogres to oversee it for her. Still, sometimes her presence is required and she reluctantly drags herself away from her work to do the tour. You stand in her retinue as she is greeted and feasted and fêted by one insignificant hamlet after another. You feel embarrassed by all those people, their bright ribbons and their singing children. Because to them this is all the world is, and you know they are a mote of dust in the world's eye. You are ashamed that your own origins are mirrored in their monkey capering. And when you look round you see Minith sneering at you, because she hasn't forgotten you're just a peasant either.

OVER THE YEARS, you become practically the house's librarian. Not of the science texts, which are still impenetrable, but Isadora has thousands of books on other subjects. You know that some are fictions, but others are histories and geographies and accounts, and you have combed these so thoroughly that you can lay your hands on any given volume someone asks for. Other staff actually come to you with questions. You are no longer the big, dumb yokel from the sticks. And Minith watches. She sits in on your conversations with Isadora, jealous still, no doubt, writing away at her own notes while you talk. She has lost her early contempt of you but maintains a distinct distance. Some people, you think, can never be won over.

And you are starting to become frustrated in your own search, because it's been years now. You've ransacked the library, and the bitter truth is that there were things the historians never wrote down. There is a shape in the middle of what happened at the Brink that nobody directly addressed.

You even talk to Minith about it, in the absence of any other options. She gives you a strange look and says, "Why do you think that is?" and you realise this, too, is part of the test. And she leaves a book by your bed – Minith being the one other person who knows the library as well as you have come to do – but it's one of the fictions, and what's the use of that?

One evening, two generals come to visit Isadora. They are big ogres, overstuffed in colourful uniforms blazing with gold braid and medals. They arrive on the backs of enormous horses and cuff and swear at Isadora's grooms. They have swords at their belts you'd need two hands to lift, and spurs jingling at their booted heels. Isadora plainly thinks they're ridiculous, but at the same time apparently they're powerful amongst the ogres. One is a duke, a very high rank indeed. They have come to discuss their requirements for the war.

You weren't aware there was a war, but apparently there is, and these two generals are currently losing. You attend your Mistress and hear them tutting over the ceded territory, the fallen soldiers. "Better stock," one says, "better weapons. We need an advantage, your ladyship, so naturally we come to you. Fine mind, eh? One of the best."

"*The* best," Isadora says, but quietly. It's plain these two clownish creatures are important, and she's on her best behaviour about them. Their moustaches bristle. Their staff look cowed and you'd bet those bright red coats conceal bruises and whip scars.

After they've gone, Isadora throws her entire staff at whatever the new project is. You ask about the war, but other than the general impression of appalling destruction and loss of life, nobody has time to talk to you about it.

Without anyone to act as your sounding board, you find yourself adrift in a morass of histories that are dancing about something in the past. In frustration, you take yourself off to one of the house's further rooms with the fiction book and read that. It is set around the Brink, you see, some romantic drama of the rich and powerful who were putting into place the changes that would save the world. Probably Minith thought it was factual, you think derisively. And yet you read it, not – you tell yourself – because you really care about any of those non-existent people, but because when you stop, your mind nags at you about what might happen next. Will the angsty daughter be happy with that troubled scion?

Will the old uncle die, and who will inherit the house? And all through the narrative, the substrate on which all those fake people stand, is the story of the Brink. How the people of the world must be changed, if they are all to live in it without devouring everything like a plague of locusts (you have to look up what a locust is). The hard decisions made by those powerful people, about altering the very book of humanity. Making it a less expensive volume to print, so the conceit of the old writer goes. Cheaper inks. Fewer pages. The paperback edition.

At no time do any of those characters step from the page to tell you what happened, but somehow the writer does. And there is a spin to the words, when talking of the Brink and What Was Done. So that, though they never have their characters say 'This was a terrible thing,' their choice of phrase invisibly coats the scenes with a sense of guilt and shame.

You look up 'hardbacks' and 'paperbacks' and page count, and disentangle the writer's metaphors of a printing industry that no longer exists in that form. Fewer pages, they said. The concise pocket edition of humanity.

You understand where the ogres came from, after that.

AND THEN YOU go to war. Not, thankfully, as a soldier, but Isadora must travel close to where the fighting is, to deliver her new inventions to the generals. She doesn't relish the task, displaying not even her usual ill temper at being dragged from her work but a particular dread you've not seen before. But her retinue travel with her, of course, you included. You go by train, one carriage for you and the one behind loaded with reinforced barrels of whatever it is that she and her staff have been cooking up. There is little talk. The trains pass through miserable-looking villages, each consisting of the same house over and over in long terraces. You see children there playing soldier games, or else they are actually being taught how to be soldiers. They have sticks over their shoulders and march back and forth. These are the villages that the generals own and they only have one use for their people. The war needs bodies. When the rails run out, you travel in big armoured cars, stuffy and dark and cramped. You meet actual soldiers. They are just staff dressed in a different uniform, these ones bright red like poor copies of the generals' own. You have seen pictures of soldiers from before the Brink. In the photographs they wore drab earth colours so they could not be seen. In even older pictures they wore bright colours like these, though, so that they could. So that their generals could look across a battlefield and see immediately where everyone was and who was on which side. Since the visit of the two generals, you have been reading up on war. Many of the soldiers don't look that much older than the children you saw from the train windows.

Soon the cars are lumbering and juddering over land that looks like the war in the photos, churned up into mud and pockmarked with holes. The soldiers still look like those in the old paintings, though, even though their bright colours are smeared with mud. You are approaching what they call the Forward HQ.

The generals are there, the two from before and a handful of others. They have a big table that has been painstakingly modelled into a map of the war, and scattered over it are thousands of little figures of soldiers in different colours. Isadora and her staff are forced to wait while some great moustache-bristling discussion is held between them, about how to stem the recent reversals. The war is going very badly. Without some new advantage, it may be lost entirely, and then where would everyone be? You want to ask that exact question, but it's abundantly plain that the generals are not like Isadora and would not appreciate a mere Economic questioning them.

At last they turn to Isadora and demand that she tell them what she's brought. The gas in the barrels and the drugs in the canisters. To affect the enemy in new and lethal ways; to empower their soldiers to fight on without fatigue or fear. The generals are delighted. This could be the turning point of the war! Their opposite numbers won't know what hit them. Victory by the end of the year, what, what?

Because there's nobody else, it's Minith you're forced to ask. "Who are we fighting?"

"*We* aren't fighting anyone," she says derisively, but then she relents and says, "If you went about thirty miles that way, you'd find another building like this one."

"Right."

"And in there, you'd find another group of generals and

another map table. Only I think that lot wear yellow, or maybe it's blue."

"Ogres?"

"Masters, yes. Of course." She's watching you carefully.

"Well then… what's the war about? What started it?" You've read your histories, about the complex skein of causes that wars arise from. "Why are the ogres fighting each other?"

But Minith is looking at you pityingly. "They're not," she says. "People are fighting each other. Because the Masters like their wars." Seeing your blank face, she says, "You know when Her Ladyship plays cards with her peers, Torquell?"

You nod.

"It's like that. Just like that."

That evening, the generals retire to their smoking room for brandy and – yes – cards and talk about how splendid this new phase of the war is going to be, and they insist Isadora accompany them, jostling over who gets to take her arm. You end up with the staff, again, only the local staff are all soldiers. Minith talks in a low voice with one older man, and you go wandering.

There is a lot of war detritus here, outside the battle proper. You get a young recruit to show you around. There are barracks where hundreds of soldiers are trying to sleep, packed in like goods in a train carriage. There is a hospital, where what seems almost the same number of soldiers lie in the same close conditions, only there are less of them – less of each one, mostly. Fewer legs and arms. And you think about that. There is an armoury where the guns are kept, because the soldiers aren't allowed to carry them until it's time to go off to battle.

You think a *lot* about that.

You meet an officer, standing outside the hospital. He's a surgeon as well, you discover, and his name is Bradwell; Captain Doctor Bradwell. He's smoking, which is something all the soldiers do. It helps with their nerves, he explains. Most of the soldiers have just looked at you dully, but Captain Doctor Bradwell has questions. Where do you come from? What's the work like there? You tell him of Her Ladyship's service, and then you tell him about the mean, filthy peasant village you're embarrassed to have come from. He listens as though you're describing paradise.

"But all good little monkeys, no doubt," he says. "Never a thought of us and what we go through?"

"They don't even know," you confirm. And then add, "But I do, now."

You lock eyes, him looking up at you, and there's a moment of connection. "Don't forget us," he tells you, and you won't. "Tell them about us," he says. You won't do that either, but perhaps you'll do something better.

Later on, there is a commotion. Shouting from the room the generals have retired to. And then a quick gathering of staff, Minith running up to drag you away from your increasingly interesting chat with Captain Doctor Bradwell.

Something has happened and you're leaving. There's already a car waiting and Isadora standing beside it. Her fury is writ large on her face, but a fury she can't give rein to. You've never seen her in a position where she can't just do whatever she wants.

Not a word, in the jolting car ride back to the train lines. In the distance you hear thunder, and then realise it's the guns of the war.

In the train, Isadora drinks. She gets through a bottle and a half before she even speaks, and then she banishes most of the staff to the far end of the carriage, has you sit beside her, and only Minith left within earshot.

"Fucking war," she says. "Fucking little boys with their toys." For all that she's been making new toys for them.

"Did they… take advantage?" Minith asks, very precisely. For a moment Isadora's eyes blaze hatred at her trim little majordomo. Then she sags massively and shudders. You were trying to keep up with what happened, between her and the generals, but even back in the village you saw this sort of thing play out. A woman and a man, and the man strong or important enough that he's hard to say no to. Not a lever you ever applied your own weight to, though opportunity certainly tempted you. And you'd heard that both Gerald Grimes and Sir Peter had a reputation for just such things, although back then you'd never have even thought to criticise such dealings. They were the ogres, after all; the Master in his castle, et cetera. But you never dreamt that such strata of power existed even amongst the ogres, or that such a grand personage as Lady Isadora could find herself in a position where she couldn't say no.

She drinks some more, trying to wash away the memories, and then she leans into you. And you're strong enough, by then, to prop her up, and for a while she just rambles about how much she loathes the generals, collectively and individually, and what a waste the whole sham-war is. Although evidently she just feels it is a distraction from the true search for knowledge; she doesn't much go into the absent limbs of the hospital or the haunted look in Captain Doctor Bradwell's eyes. She talks about the 'proper use' of the Economics, the rational duties of a responsible owner. And then she prods you in the chest and demands, "Have you worked it out, then? All your reading. You must have, by now."

She's not really expecting an answer, already having you refill her glass, but as you hand it to her you say, "Yes."

Her eyes sparkle with sudden interest, a slice of her old mischief. "And?"

And you tell her where the ogres come from. Or rather, that they never came from anywhere. That all those histories of the Brink, lovingly detailing the hard decisions made by the powerful people, about how they would save the world, omitted one key element: that they excluded themselves from those measures.

"When it's consumption of resources that's the issue," you say, "then 'economic' just means smaller. That's us. You stayed the same."

She's smiling, and partly it's the 'good boy' response to a pet who can perform a new trick, but there's her old slyness there as well, because you're almost right, but there's one piece of the puzzle left over.

"A handful of genes to control height and size," she

murmurs, slurring a little. "Easier than you think. A handful of genes to control diet, which proteins can be digested, which can't. That's trickier. Your father still enjoyed a boiled egg and a glass of milk, probably. Some bloodlines still do. Not"—she belches—"an exact science, quite. A handful of genes to lower testosterone and other truculent hormones. More manageable, eh? All to save the world from the teeming hordes. But you haven't guessed it." She sounds like a spoiled child who didn't get a pony for her birthday. "I was sure you'd have worked it out by now."

And you're blank. You've dropped your grand revelation, but apparently that's not it.

When you get back, you spend plenty of time staring at the books, but the last secret isn't in there. Nobody wrote a book about *you*, after all. And all the while, what you saw in the war zone is festering in you. What you saw in the slums around the city. And, scrape down far enough, there's your own personal experience. The dogs, and Gerald, and your father. And the strange thing is, despite it all, you do like Isadora. And you can tell yourself, *she's better than the others*. She doesn't whip her staff. She treats them well and brings out the best in them. If you had to be any ogre's pet, then there would be no better Master than her.

But that *If*. A word that would have been unthinkable back when you lived in the village. Unthinkable in your early years as Isadora's tame peasant. But you've read now. You understand about the Brink. It's true, as the pastor always said, that the world was ordained this way. But not by God. And with God out of the equation, that leaves room for the question, *What if it wasn't this way?*

And one evening, Minith comes to the library, leaning in the doorway as you tread back through books you've already exhausted, needling through the haystack to find what you missed.

Your glower only amuses her. You'd have thought she'd approve, finding you here burning the midnight oil amongst these pages, but apparently that's just more food for the contempt that never really left her.

"You're so blind," she tells you. "You're looking two hundred years back in time and you never see the here and now. You missed dinner, didn't you?"

You did, and you're hungry. Sheer stubbornness is keeping you at this fruitless study.

"Go ask the cooks to heat you up something," she tells you imperiously, and then adds. "After all, nobody else will have had it."

You blink at her. There's far too much mockery in that smile for her words not to mean *something* beyond the obvious.

"Tell me," you demand, but she won't. She just says, "You never watch the cooks at work, do you?"

You eat. You sleep. Next day you watch the cooks as they make lunch. Your lunch, and the staff's lunch. Separately. Every meal for years, this has been going on, but you were always too good for the kitchen. Why would you ever have sat there, a volume unregarded on your knees, watching them make food for the staff and Her Ladyship and for you? And mostly you eat what the staff get, but with an added ingredient. A little of what Isadora has, minced up and baked into whatever's going. Meat from her own table. Nothing but the best.

And you remember a word that was used, a handful of times long ago, when referring to you.

You go back to the library and, for the first time in many months, look up the meaning of something in the dictionaries. You search out the definition of *atavism*.

CHAPTER SEVEN

AFTER THAT, THINGS can't be the same. You look in the mirror, and what looks back at you is like one of those pictures you've seen, the vase that is the two faces, the duck that is the rabbit facing the other way. *What am I?* But now everything makes sense: your riotous childhood, your temper, Gerald's death. And that newly reinterpreted past must surely lead to a different future to the one you had planned. You've a destiny, if you could only work out what it is.

 Isadora calls you to attend that evening. She is still seething about the generals and their cavalier treatment of her. She drinks and swears and throws a wineglass across the room. Then she calls you to her and tells you how fond of you she is, holds you to her bosom, tousles your hair. But you feel all those strings that bind you to her, gratitude and servitude, fraying and snapping. And she doesn't notice because she doesn't concern herself with the moods of servants.

You know, by the time she retires to bed, that you can't stay. You are not her pet any more. You were born for another purpose, because you were born different. Your father was cuckolded by genetics, and you are something more than just a village headman's son.

Late that night, you gather everything you will need. You abandon the histories that have sustained you for years and take more current reading: maps, and plans of the train network especially. You fill a pack with spare clothes and food from the kitchens, and you take other things too, whatever you can lay hands on that will help. And you are as sly and subtle as you can be, but it's not enough. You are seen, and perhaps that's because certain eyes were expecting it.

And you creep from the house, looking back just once with a little pang of conscience, because Isadora was good to you, in her own way. She has given you this second childhood, to let you grow into who you need to be. But as with all children, one day you must strike out on your own. You have great things to accomplish.

You cross the grounds towards the estate's wall and gate. To your own surprise, you don't feel nervous at all. That fear belongs to the man you thought you were, not the man you now know yourself to be.

Some of the staff patrol the grounds at night, but you wait till they've gone by and until the man slouching by the gate is either called away, or gets bored, or needs to piss. You stand before the great iron portal topped with barbed wire thorns and find it locked.

You're stronger and fitter than you ever used to be, after the full meals – the full and *meaty* meals – you've been eating these last years, but the gates offer few footholds and the barbs atop them look savage. Easier than the wall, though, and you take a few steps back, ready to make your run up and hope the sound doesn't wake everyone back in the house.

And they open. Of their own accord. Giving you a view of the formless darkness beyond: your destiny. You realise you're being watched.

It's Minith, standing there in the moonlight in her white uniform. She holds some device, presumably the control for the gate. You had counted on being a long way from the house before anybody marked your absence. For a long heartbeat you stare at each other.

Her pointed face is closed, but you see her nod and the gate is open. A blessing, of sorts, and you can't work out why. She has never concealed her dislike of you. But then that dislike is rooted in your monopolising her Mistress's time, displacing her as the most favoured of the favoured few. And now you're going. No more will you be standing between her and advancement.

She watches still, as you cross through the gate, a Rubicon (you came across the word in a book, and understand its meaning even if you don't know its origin) you cannot take back. And then you drop out of her sight, and she is gone from yours, and still her voice is not raised to accuse you. She is merely glad you have gone, for her own selfish reasons.

You are a fugitive again, after so many years, and you make sure that, by dawn, you are a long way from Hypatian. Specifically, by dawn you are on a train, eating sparingly from your provisions and hidden amongst the freight. The greatest thing you have equipped yourself with is not in your pack; it is an understanding of how the world works. Last time you just ran into the forest, clueless and panicking. Now, you can travel a hundred miles in an hour. Now you have a map showing countless ogre holdings and outbuildings, hunting lodges and getaways, most of which are empty or have just a skeleton staff. And more than that, you have self-knowledge.

You are going home.

Or that's the plan. You ride the train lines as close as you can to your home territory, the estates of the Grimes family, and your innocent intent is just to get within sight of the village and see how the land lies. You don't quite have a plan yet, though ideas are coagulating within your skull.

Instead, you meet Sir Peter.

You don't know whether it's blind chance that brings the two of you together, or if the old landlord is more busy about his holdings now his eldest is dead. You come across his car parked at the side of the track, a handful of servants playing a bored game of dice as they wait for their master to return. You imagine he's been out shooting, but on closer inspection there are a couple of long guns still in the back of the car. Then Sir Peter himself makes an appearance, shouldering out of the undergrowth and making his people leap up, dice scattering. There is a girl. A human girl, some village child. She is weeping and her dress is bloody and at the same time she is trying desperately to appear grateful and happy and obedient. So...

You don't *decide* to step out into the open, but that is what you've done, you find. And Sir Peter's reaction is all you could possibly want. His face goes purple and his eyes pop and you think for a moment he will die on the spot. He hasn't forgotten you: how you took his son after he'd taken your father; how you were ripped from the claws of his justice. You see on his face how that has festered with him ever since. And now you're here.

He snarls for his people to take you, his beaters. They try. You break one's arm and throw the next so hard he can only wheeze for breath. The remaining two are terrified of you. Because you're angry and strong and bigger than them, and because where that spark of rage should be in them, there's just a hole. They were engineered that way. It makes them more Economic.

Sir Peter has gone for the gun case, but you slap it from his hands, spilling the oiled-metal contents to the earth. He raises his stick.

You take it from him. This wasn't what you came here to do, but as you feel the solid weight of it in your hand, you realise it *was*. This is where your destiny takes you. Of course this day was coming.

You strike Sir Peter with his own cane, the brass hawk's-head handle gouging across his face. The sound that comes from his servants is that of worshippers seeing their god's idol pulled down.

He screeches: not pain, not anger, but indignation. How *dare* you? But you dare more than that. You haven't finished with him. You beat him again and again, and the third blow catches him in the head and he goes down. His new stick is well-made. It doesn't break. It outlasts his skull and his brains.

The beaters and the other staff haven't made a move to stop you. They stare in horror as you fill your pack with food from Sir Peter's hamper and take the gun case, heaving its weight of weapons and shot over your shoulder by its strap. Only then does one of them make a token effort at getting in your way, as though the theft of the property is somehow the final straw. But a look dissuades that man, and you are off into the woods, walking jauntily with the hawk's-head stick and a clearer idea of what you're going to do. You were wrong. Breaching the wall of Hypatian wasn't your Rubicon. Sir Peter's skull has fulfilled that function.

Two of them follow you, plus the girl Sir Peter had been dallying with. You keep an eye on them, don't acknowledge them, until you're deep in the woods and have started a fire with the lighter you brought from Hypatian. Then they creep out warily, as though you'll turn your rage on them, but you invite them to share the fire, and give them such food as they can eat. Sir Peter's people's names are Serge and Potto; the girl's is Layla. She tells you about her home, a village you've vaguely heard of, and the recent bad harvest and Sir Peter's taxes and penalties and punishments. Serge and Potto half-tell, half-show by their manner, that they are lovers, and that Sir Peter has had both of them whipped, for that reason and for others.

You give them all the chance to abandon you. Sir Peter's death will stir a howling response from the ogres. But they have seen something in you. You are, after all, a hero, and you are coming into your kingdom.

The next day, Layla goes to her home and asks until she finds someone who knows of a band of outlaws in the woods, and where they might be found, and you go with your own little band of followers to meet Roben again, after all this time.

THE YEARS HAVE made Roben older, while they seem only to have made you more vital, as though the energy time leaches out of everyone else has found a home in you. You do not remember any of the rest of his band. But it is Roben, though, who Layla takes you to. The old man's canny enough that he's still in charge of his band. And that band is three times the size it was, you can see. The years haven't been kind to the lands under Sir Peter's care, and neither has Sir Peter. And maybe that's your doing, indirectly, or maybe things would always have gone that way. You certainly can't imagine things being kinder if it were Gerald making the rounds now, rather than Grimes Senior.

You walk into the circle of his fire, and he sees you and your name spills from his lips, and half your work's done in that moment.

Because they remember you. They remember you as dead, and doubtless in the villages they cast you as a devil and a monster, scourged by the pastor every church-day. But to the outlaws you became something else. They must have someone to hate for the cold nights and the lean days, after all, and so they hate the ogres, secure in the knowledge that they will never be in a position to act on that hate; it remains merely something to keep in their shrivelled bellies when the foraging is poor. And you are the man who killed an ogre. And you died.

And here you are.

You sit down at the fire and greet Roben with your old boyish smile, and you introduce Layla and Potto and Serge, and you get out the food you took from Sir Peter's car. The bread and the fruit and other good things get passed round the circle. The cold meats, the sausages, you keep for yourself. They watch you tear into them with a fearful fascination.

You tell them the first version of your great speech, then. You've tried to think it out, but despite all those books, you're someone who gets better by doing, so it's as well you have such a primed audience. You tell them the Truth, though it's a Truth with the complex edges rounded off until it's something small and simple enough to swallow. You tell them the thing they always told themselves bitterly, when the fire guttered low and the frost lay on the ground: that the ogres are no better than them. The thing they told each other and never believed, but which is true.

They tricked your ancestors, you say. They stole something from them, but kept it for themselves. You speak of the Brink, the genetic engineering, the whole salutary story of saving the world that the books taught you. But you turn it round. You tell a history omitted by the winners. It becomes a kind of creation myth, a story of the before-times when there was only one people, and how *they* cheated *us*. And where you stand, one foot across the *them-us* divide, you do not say, but you are here, back from the dead, and though there is no logical correlation there, that somehow stands as proof.

You tell them what happened to Sir Peter, and though you see Roben's face go troubled, more than half those around the fire are cheering you on then, and who cares who hears? The old ogre has indeed been upping the taxes and the beatings since you killed his son. He has, all unknowing, been preparing his people for your triumphant return.

"They will not let that go," Roben says eventually. A wise old man after all, and not unmoved by what you've said, but he takes his responsibilities seriously. A man over-cautious to be captain, but a good lieutenant, you think.

"They will not," you agree. "The servants of his who lived, they will have spread the word already. There will be ogres, and then there will be dogs." And you shiver despite yourself, remembering Theo; remembering Catch and Tongs.

You see Roben make the necessary calculations. If there are dogs, they will track you here, to where the scent of all his people will be spread out like a picnic for them to sample. He is about to give his usual order, the one he gave when you turned up with Gerald's blood on your hands: flee, use the water, go plague the outskirts of some other village. Hope they will stop looking. Except, as you know from last time, they won't, and these measures won't work.

You stand up before he can commit himself. "Listen to me," you tell them. "You think I came back just to kill the man who murdered my father? You think that's it and I'm done?" A precisely weighted beat before you go on. "You think I'd leave all of you?"

"All of who?" Roben demands, as you knew he would.

"Everyone. The real people. Those who suffer under the ogres' boot. You, every one of you. The people in the villages. All the others I've seen, these last years."

It's too big for a lot of them. Roben sees, though. Even though he's shaking his head, you know he had those same thoughts once, maybe when he first turned outlaw. And he gave them up in exchange for just surviving one year at a time. But then, he's not a hero like you.

"Piss on what the pastor preaches," you tell them. "Nothing put them over us but their own trickery. And they're not better than us. And we don't need them. They need us. Without us, who tills their fields, who works in their factories, who fights their play-wars?" And they don't really understand those last things, but you're already planning ahead.

And some say nobody from the villages will care – since the outlaws have fled village justice, for the most part.

Others still have the Master in his Castle whipped deep into them. And still more just harbour plain fear.

But you tell them, "I am going to the House." And there is only one 'House': Sir Peter's. "I am going to take from it everything I choose and turn his family out onto the road, just like you were all turned out. And then I will burn it down. Because the death of one landlord is not enough of a message to send to the ogres, nor it is punishment enough for the crimes of their forebears. Who's with me?"

And you make it perfectly clear, in your tone, that you will go alone if you have to, and will still triumph, no matter the odds. And because of that, men and women around the fire start standing up and pledging themselves to the venture. They're the younger ones, generally; the ones most recently turned off their land and out of their homes. In many cases, they were cast out of their villages for good reason. People for whom the chance to rob a big house is more important than generations of injustice. Right now you can't be choosy about who follows you. You offer absolution for any who will stand beneath your banner.

And you look at Roben, waiting to see which way he will run. You've come and taken his people from him, and taken his choices, and that's wrong. He didn't deserve that, the man who was always a friend to you. But you've given him something, too; cast it at his feet, if he'll only pick it up. You've given him hope and a purpose and the truth.

And you think he'll just stay sat at his fire, and then you think he'll walk away, a band of one under the merry greenwood. But when he stands, stiffly, it's not to go anywhere. No words, for that would bind him to you more than he can stand, but a nod, just like Minith's nod.

A FEW DAYS on the road, to Sir Peter's big house. You had twenty when you left Roben's camp. You have thirty-three when you reach the high walls and the big gates. Roben has people out scavenging and scrounging, living off the land as you must. Nobody keeps their mouth shut; word spreads. Doubtless there are agitated committees of village elders talking about what must be done, but the disaffected and the young don't talk. They just come and find you on the road and join in. There are those who were hovering on the point of outlawry already. There are even a couple who know their letters and have thought about the world and know injustice when they see it.

A high wall runs all the way around the extensive grounds, but nobody has challenged Sir Peter or his peers in generations, and so the maintenance of that wall isn't all it should be. Serge shows you where he knows a tree that has grown up until its branches overshadow the wall top. You consider cameras and surveillance, but Potto and Serge, who once called this place home, tell you the staff barely pay any attention to such systems. When were they last needed, after all?

You're over the wall and advancing on the house. And probably there are servants on patrol, perhaps with dogs, but if so, they are few and far between and the grounds are huge. You meet none of them.

The house is all lit up, burning a wealth of energy in its chandeliers and lamps. You and Roben and a handful of others creep forward to scout the bright windows and see what's what.

You're expecting a staff of maybe twenty, and Sir Peter's wife and any resident children. Instead, there are a full half-dozen ogres thronging the drawing room, windows thrown open to let out the fuming fug of their cigar smoke and sweat and alcohol. The one woman you take to be Mrs Grimes. She is nominally hostess, but you know the dynamics of ogre gatherings and you see she has no control of this one. They are all big men, dressed much as Sir Peter was – his peers, neighbouring landlords. They are drunk, and one of them sits very close to Mrs Grimes, his hand on her leg, his mouth speaking condolences but his eyes saying very different things. For a moment you are startled that the house is host to a party with Sir Peter's brains so recently dashed onto the road, but then you understand his death is the cause. This is a band of gallant hunters, assembled here before heading out to track you down. They are stuffed with declarations, telling each other what they will do to you, and every other monkey they can catch. They will exhibit your mutilated body in every village. They will make you eat your own excrement and then your own hands. They roar with laughter at their inventiveness.

You creep back to the main body of your army and give your orders.

The first the ogres know of the attack is almost the last.

You swarm in through the windows, you and your people. Your followers lack the berserker's fire; it was stolen from their inheritance. They can feel angry but they cannot really *rage*. But you lead them, and you have knives, and you have Sir Peter's gun that blows a hole in the first ogre to stand up. And sometimes you don't need a full-on fury to get violent. The villages are full of slapped children and beaten wives and men with missing teeth and black eyes, after all. Sometimes the screw of frustration can be turned enough that it compensates for the dampened serotonin and testosterone.

Your people have clubs and staves, mostly, and little knives and wood hatchets. The ogres have their vast strength and the fuel of their outrage. Your followers could have been easily cowed, had the ogres been given a chance. But you are not cowed, and you lead by example. You strike the first blow, and then your people are swarming desperately about the room, hacking at the giants in a death of a thousand cuts and a hundred blows. And some of the house staff are sufficiently loyal that they try to intervene – mostly those, like the beaters, who have been shaped into little ogres themselves, dwarfish mockeries of their masters. And they die too. You told your people not to kill the servants, but self-defence is self-defence. And you told them to spare Mrs Grimes, too, and this they do. The huge woman is backed into a corner, shielding herself, a cat bearded by mice. And because of that, she lives.

And then the ogres, who had so recently been boasting of how they'd make your last hours a torment, are dead, and the room is ankle-deep in their vast reserves of blood, and the house is yours.

Your people want to celebrate, but there's no time for that. Mrs Grimes is locked in the cellar, along with three ogre children of varying ages, and the majority of the surviving staff, save for half a dozen who join Potto and Serge in your army.

You ransack the house for everything that you can use, and everything anybody wants. There is an abundance of carriages and cars around the front of the house, property of the various hunting ogres who came to avenge Sir Peter. Potto can drive, as can one of the others. You load up food from the pantry, knives, all the guns the intrepid hunters brought – even though they are mostly so large they'd break the shoulder of any human who fired one. You take all the spare clothing and blankets and sheets you can find. You take spare fuel for the cars, save for some that is splashed through the rooms of the house. And while the others are about this, you find Sir Peter's library. It consists of precisely nine books, six of which concern hunting, shooting and fishing, but there is a dictionary and there is a book of maps and one of natural history, and you take them all.

Then you have the Grimes family and their remaining loyalists brought out in front of the house, and you have them watch while you put a match to their ancestral pile. You burn their heritage, just like their ancestors pillaged yours. You all stand and watch the flames devour that grand old house and its priceless furniture and paintings and all the generations and years and days of their family and their lives. And Mrs Grimes weeps and squalls and shrieks at you, and your people cheer you to the heavens.

You and your band drive off in your stolen convoy, and leave them with nothing but the clothes on their backs, and consider it just.

THEY SEND THEO after you.

There is certainly a wider ogre response being formed, but sheer shock means it's slow and disjointed. This has never happened before. It is the specific thing they did their level best to preclude from their future, when they were taking steps to tackle the Brink. But Theo is an enterprising individual, and he's always been on the outside of ogre society. He doesn't fit with them any more than you fit with regular people. Of course he comes for you.

One day you hear he's in the area. Catch and Tongs track you down that night. You are waiting when they come slavering out of the trees towards you, desperate to take you in their jaws and hold you for their master.

And, because they are dogs, and you are human, they go into the pit you had dug for them. You hear them snarling and leaping and complaining down there, and they almost get out, Catch on the back of Tongs and leaping taller than a man's height. For a heartbeat the whole business is that close to unravelling. But the pit holds them, just.

Theo slouches into the clearing after, carrying a knife and a gun and staring at you. He marks the fate of the dogs, and stops with the pit between you.

"You," he murmurs. "It *is* you." Something like wonder crosses his broad ogre face. "I never had to hunt someone down twice before." The moon glints on his tusks. "What now, monkey?" He hefts his long gun, but you know he'll have been tasked to bring you in alive. So they can kill you properly, just like before. You didn't die then; you won't now.

"You're not like the other ogres," you tell him. He snarls at the name, because of course the ogres don't refer to *themselves* as that. "I thought about asking you to join me, even."

His eyes go wide, and not with the derisive mockery you expected, either. And you wonder, then, whether it actually *is* an option. Would Theo go renegade, just for the joy of the hunt? But no: he's an ogre, first and foremost, and he's made a living out of hunting and killing your kind.

"You're a clever monkey," he tells you. "You ain't all that, though. The only point of you is to make me rich." He begins stalking round the pit's edge cautiously, prodding at the ground with his gun barrel. And you think about the workers crammed into the factory slums, desperately scrabbling for wages that they only need because their masters, who want for nothing, have decreed that their world must work that way. And you wonder if this hulking ogre is trapped in just the same net. This is what happens to ogres who won't play proper ogre games.

When they tell the story later, it's you and Theo knife to knife, his brute strength against your speed until you bury your blade in his throat. What actually happens is that you take out the pistol you got from one of the ogre hunters. You don't need to bring Theo in alive, after all. His eyes go wide and he drags his own gun up, but you empty yours in a rolling tide of thunder, and an ogre is a big target. You sprain your wrist, but you are bigger than any regular human, and strong, and you've learned how to hold a gun even if you've not fired one before. Sir Peter had books about it.

In the echoes, the woods are silent save for a questioning whimper from the dogs in the pit. Then the cheering begins.

CHAPTER EIGHT

THINGS ACCELERATE BEYOND anybody's control.

The first month of the conflict is covered by a fog of ignorance on both sides. The expected instant reprisal from the ogres doesn't happen, and you personally can't understand why. What you find out later, once you've been on your travels, is that various of the ogres who might otherwise have come to quick action are arguing amongst themselves. There is considerable scoffing and doubt amongst the Masters about what has actually happened. Some see treachery amongst their own kind. Others see advantage. What mostly happens, when the Widow Grimes turns up with her depleted staff and children, demanding justice, is an inheritance dispute. Sir Peter's estates are valuable, hence a number of his neighbours begin jostling over who should be the one to console the widow and control the holdings. And, since taking a pack of beaters in to clear out the rabble would grant the form of possession which remains nine-tenths of ogre law, they all block each other's attempts to do so. A joint task force is proposed but repeatedly sunk by their machinations against each other. A couple of them try to go behind the backs of the others and just march a pack of retainers in to hunt you down, but by then you have more than enough followers to deal with them, because you've been recruiting.

Let's be frank: you're not free of your own divisions and factions. You solve the problem by never ceasing to move forwards. You expand your range and your influence, and just keep pushing because, at some level, you understand that to consolidate now would be to stagnate. It would be to sit at the fire and have people ask you the question 'What now?' It would be to have them consider the very real likelihood that any day the ogres will get their act together and come to kill you all. To you, knowing what you do of the ogres, it seems inevitable. And nobody can say what thoughts circle within you, that you never speak to another soul, but perhaps there are two wolves, and one is the hunter and the other the hunted. The hunted wolf knows it is doomed, but the hunter knows it is *right*. And, so long as you hunt, you don't need to listen to that mournful other voice.

You and Roben tour the villages, just as Sir Peter did. You even collect taxes: less than the ogres demanded even though you have more mouths to feed. Beyond this, you collect recruits. And perhaps it's not so many, in those little communities like the one where you grew up. Even though Sir Peter turned the screws on them these last few years, they are not so hard done by, and they are so, so ignorant. They believe in the hymns they sing and in the way they're told the world works. It's comforting, that belief. You remember it yourself. And yet you displace pastors and get up in the pulpit on church-days. You give them the Truth, and let them decide what to do with it. And there's always a trickle of disaffected youth and bitter elders who come with you, each time.

That's nothing to the cities.

You and a few others stow away on a train and go to the town of slums and smoke and factories that Isadora took you to, and there you find your work half-done. Because they *do* have it bad, in the tenements and the factories, and there is a long underground tradition of trying to organise and fight the bosses, to protest for better conditions, shorter hours, safer machines. And yet they were all just the same slaves to a creed as the farmers. They have demanded for generations: *can it not be slightly better for us?* and been slapped down by the truncheon-wielding thugs the ogres employ as law-keepers. And then you arrive, and tell them that their entire bubble world is like a pot, only hot and seething because someone's keeping the fire beneath it stoked. The question they should have been asking is, *why is it like this at all?* And you tell them your Truth, of the Brink and the trick the ogres pulled, and it goes through all their networks like wildfire. The ogres have set up their pressure-cooker cities so that it's work or die, and you come to them and say, *what if... neither?*

And of course there are always informers and traitors, and the police come in to break everything up. You join the workers in their fights; you crack some heads and put bullets into others. You become the terror of the law-keepers because you have seen the rot behind their badges and their laws. And because you're bigger than any of them, of course. And then you go to the big house of the ogre who gives them their orders and you leave him with his throat cut.

You have set fires across the city, literally and ideologically. You have a great swathe of new recruits, and they work in factories that make clothing and food and tools. They work in factories that make machines that can talk to each other at a distance. They can operate transport vehicles. And some of them work in the factory that makes human-sized weapons for the generals, and when you leave the city it's in a big convoy bristling with guns. Guns nobody knows much how to use, but it's a start.

And every day you wake up expecting things to be over. Because they're the *ogres*. The *Masters*. Nobody does this. Even you, who've looked behind the curtain, understands that revolutions against ultimate power end only one way. You're reminded of old stories from ogre libraries, about the wicked servant that rebels against his omnipotent master. And you know that the ogres have no mandate from God, but you also know that, given the time to get themselves into gear, they won't need one.

* * *

You get back, with your new recruits and your new resources, to find that the generals have finally taken over, amongst the ogres. They have been playing their war games for generations, after all. Now you've given them an excuse to take their games out of the mud-churned stretches of no man's land set aside for their frolics. The old war is over, long live the new war. The war against Torquell.

Not that they know your name. You'll learn later that they've yet to connect you with the boy who killed Gerald Grimes years ago, let alone Isadora's hulking protégé. The monkey rebellion in Sir Peter's lands is just a headless, formless outrage. And an excuse for the generals to play on a bigger map.

There are eyes in the sky now. The ogre generals were always keen on watching their toy wars, seeing the explosions and the doomed charges into the cannon's mouth. But those eyes are designed for the mud and the wire, not your forests. When they come low enough to get under the canopy, they're easy prey for stones and bullets. And, perhaps, those eyes are not as sharp as the ogres believe. Perhaps not always looking in the right direction. Sometimes, they wink.

You get visitors to your camp. Captain Doctor Bradwell and a handful of others whose rank or role lets them move more freely. Men who can influence just where those eyes are looking. You get voices whispering to you, over the radios you liberated from the factories, as your new recruits train in marksmanship. And most of the time, the red-coated patrols sent to track you down find only cold ashes of campfires, or letters pinned to trees telling them the Truth, that they mostly burn but sometimes read. Or sometimes they find pits and traps, ambushes, sabotage. Certain squads more zealous in their obedience to ogre orders just don't return at all. And you keep their vehicles and their weapons.

Sometimes they take villages, scorch earth, evict everyone in a great tantrum, and every time they do, you gain new recruits and new zeal, people who see through the ogre lie. And you have raided the food processing plants of their cities, and your supply lines are sturdier than theirs. You hear the toll of charred houses and deaths and know it's all to your advantage.

They set up artillery and blow up patches of woodland that you swiftly evacuate or that you knew not to be in. And some nights you lead your people to where you've been tipped off those guns have been set, and you turn the guns on the next artillery emplacement over, or just cart them off for your own use.

But no matter how many weapons you keep, the big set-piece battle the ogre generals are hankering for never happens. You have few good shots amongst your people, and nobody has strong nerves. The white-hot fury that you feel, when you think about the Truth and the Brink, is a low fire in all the others. They can't help it. They were engineered that way, so as not to be able to stand up to their Masters. There are no lions amongst them, and so you fight a mouse's war, creeping and hiding and avoiding confrontation unless the odds are stacked in your favour. Because even a mouse can pull a trigger.

And every night you wonder that they haven't crushed you. And every dawn there's new information that's seeped out of the army camp, about where they'll go next, and who they'll send. To the generals, you're magically one step ahead of them all the time, and they grow frustrated. Their war game isn't fun to play any more when it's not their own kind calling the shots on both sides.

One general loses his temper entirely, just gathers up a hasty force and leads it into the forest himself. And, because it's done on a whim and without planning, you get almost no warning, and there is a battle then. A fight, strung out through the merry greenwood. And the soldiers wear bright red coats, and your people wear peasant brown or factory grey. And you know the woods, while they just know mud and trenches.

You make yourself a target. You're a fool. If a bullet found you, that day, it would all fall apart. But your followers fight because you're there, in their midst, and perhaps if you'd hidden behind the lines they'd have broken and fled.

And by then you outnumber the expeditionary force more than four to one, men and women with the same rifles they give the soldiers, with a handful of armoured vehicles, and with trucks and cars and tracked construction machinery. And some of the soldiers have taken off their red coats anyway, joining you, or just fleeing, because this isn't the war they signed up for. Because the letters you left them opened their eyes to the possibility of not fighting any war at all. And you surround the rest, deep in the woods, like the savage tribesmen of another age encircled the legions of a long-gone imperial power. You take their guns, and then you have the ogre general brought to you. You face him with Catch on one side and Tongs on the other, because while you were in the city, Roben was showing Theo's dogs a little kindness.

There are a hundred ways you can take things from here, but in your mind is the knowledge that the moment you cease to move forwards, cease to escalate, you're lost. And so you send the general's head back to his peers along with those soldiers who still want to follow ogre orders. And many of them don't, now you've defeated them. They know that going back as losers will see beatings and punishments and executions by firing squad, because the ogres only know one way of motivating their human troops. And they hear the Truth from your lips, and you light the little fire in them that you've been setting everywhere you go.

The head, sent back, finally convinces the ogres that they aren't playing a game anymore. This isn't a jolly hunting expedition or a chance for the generals to play at war. This is insurrection, and it's spreading. Factories have burned, cities have been overturned. Whole districts and villages, counties, boroughs are being overseen by your lieutenants, rather than the ogres or their minions.

And so the news comes to you that they've stopped playing around.

Nobody else understands, amongst your people. Only

you had the years of leisure in Isadora's library reading about the Brink and the times before.

The people of that suffocatingly crowded world were skilled at war, meaning they devised many ways of conducting war that did not require human intervention. They had machines that flew and spied out the land for them, and they had bullets that could be launched from many miles away to destroy a whole village. They had aircraft as swift as the wind with bellies full of death. They had weapons that brought plague, and weapons that were just air, except the air killed too. And they had regular tools of soldiery beyond the dreams of the poor soldiers the ogre generals have been unleashing on you, and their soldiers' coats weren't bright red either. Or not in the immediately pre-Brink times. The historical model the ogres revert to is an older and more visceral one. You cannot play war games with the technology of the pre-Brink days because the games would be over too quickly. In fact, since pulling the world back from the Brink – or at least since the clean-up immediately after that – the world has not needed the old model of war. The ogres have their disagreements, but they are all of a class and a society together and there are other ways they can push and shove. Perhaps this is one blessing of the terrible things they did.

But you – you have finally achieved something. You have brought the old war back. The weapons have been broken out of mothballs and rushed to a command post some way distant from the woods, a compromise between their knowing they can exterminate you from the horizon, and them wanting to see the flames and smell the smoke themselves. Ogres are creatures of appetite, after all. They did not render themselves immune to the lessening that saved the world from the Brink only to deny their desires later. They do not just want to kill you, or even to know that you are dead. They want to *see* it, and celebrate it. They want your head above the mantelpiece, or your body swinging in a city square as a warning to others.

You hear whispers on the radio of what they have. Vehicles with many missiles; missiles with minds that can identify their own targets; canisters of toxins; gas masks. The new soldiers have been issued with new uniforms of brown and green.

And you, the *Atavism*, are ogre enough that you, too, must go see for yourself.

You pick a task force, everyone who can fit in your vehicle fleet. This is your throw of the dice, no sense holding back. The rest you tell to scatter, and if you don't come back, then they should find somewhere, some slum, some distant village. It will be over, if you don't come back. You know this fact with an unfailing certainty: you *are* the rebellion.

And you remember other histories, from long before the Brink. Of upstart slaves crucified in long lines along straight roads; of barricades torn down and students shot. This is how revolutions end, most of the time. The path you've trodden isn't new, and you always understood where it would likely lead. But when you knew enough about the world, what was done in the past and what you were, what other choice was left to you? You're a hero, after all. A hero doesn't stand idly by. He gets *involved*, no matter the cost.

You expect, any moment, the faceless death that the Brink weapons can deal. Your entire force can be wiped out at the ogres' pleasure, and they must know you are coming. Or perhaps they have a vast number of monkeys puzzling over many user manuals, trying to remember how this sort of war is assembled and set into motion.

As your force nears the camp, as the skies grow grey with the first breath of morning, you can hear the shooting, but by the time you reach their perimeter fence – along the path not seeded with mines, thanks to the whisperings of the radio – it is over.

In the centre of the camp are many soldiers, some wounded, all disarmed, and in the centre of them, nine ogres. More generals, still in their medal-bedecked bright uniforms because they weren't going to be the ones who went out into the woods to mop up the last of the resistance. And surrounding these unfortunates is the army.

Just as with the villages under Sir Peter's hard hand; just as with the cities where the squeezing of the factory-mongers meant that, when you cut them an exit, they were ready to erupt through it; just as with every step of your life, it's as though events were only waiting for a hero like you to come along. You stride into the army camp through doors the soldiers throw open for you. Catch and Tongs pad alongside you, and you're wearing a long grey coat one of your people made to your outsize measurements that has something of the soldier to it. And Captain Doctor Bradwell, in charge of the insurrection, salutes you because he's a soldier and that's what soldiers do. And you salute back, and from that moment you're a general. You see the ogres note this exchange and their huge eyes are wide with real fear.

You take their gifts, all the real weapons from the real wars rather than the toys they have been playing with ever since. You will have to spend time puzzling over the books and the electronic documents and the rest before you can use any of it. Much of it you perhaps will never be able to use, or will find too dangerous to play with. But it's yours, and more to the point, the other ogres know you have it. And it wasn't as if they particularly remembered how to use those weapons either. There's a parity of ignorance.

You stand before the generals, and they rant at you. They curse and spit at Bradwell and his fellow members of the junta. They invoke law and privilege and the chain of command. And when they have exhausted their rhetoric and lowered themselves in the eyes of those who stayed loyal to them, you stand up and tell the Truth again. You're good at it now. The words come out with smooth assurance, with an orator's aim to fly true and pierce an armoured heart. You tell the soldiers about how their ancestors were robbed and cheated, and at least half change their minds about whose side they want to be on.

The rest you send back with nothing but their boots and uniforms. Bradwell and some of the others advise you to hold them or take more drastic steps, but you're not that far along the road yet. The generals, though, you have shot, just the same firing squad they'd ordain for any of their soldiers who turned against them. When the salvo of rifle fire has resounded, you walk forwards and put a bullet into the sagging head of each gigantic monster, before the eyes of your new army.

AFTER THAT, IT'S mostly logistics for a while. You have become good at delegating. Anyone who has a penchant for organisation has a leg-up to advancement from you. You've read books. You know that armies are not just guns and battles, but meals and billets and morale. And by now you have to accept that what you are in charge of isn't just an army; it's a community. Men, women and children farming and making and mending and cooking and *living*. The edges of your realm are all drilling and trying to understand the user manuals, but the centre is slowly crystallising into something stable, where life can actually go on.

And you know it won't last. The ogres haven't immediately rained death from the sky over you; they're a little stunned at all the reversals, you suspect. But whatever the illusion of permanence in the centre, you know you have to keep pushing outwards. Stagnate, and they will get over their surprise and come to destroy everything. You keep sending people to the next village, the next city. You get word from the infiltrators who went back with the defeated soldiers. You keep pushing. And still the ogres are like fog. No new army gets sent to oppose you. No ballistic missiles leap up from past the horizon. The ogres are trying something new, and no whispers come to tell you what it is.

Until, one day, a car races up to your forward command post, and instead of news it brings a prisoner; a messenger, in fact.

It's Minith, whom you haven't seen for more than half a year, not since you stepped through the gate of Hypatian to begin your career as a doomed revolutionary.

The ogres want to talk. Isadora wants to talk.

CHAPTER NINE

"She thinks I'll trust her," you say to Minith.

"Don't you?" is her reply.

She's remarkably bold, there in the heart of your army, but she always did have a high opinion of herself. Confidence is armour, up to a point.

And you're thinking about Isadora. Who is an ogress, yes, but you spent six years in her house. As her servant, her property, her *pet*, but still… She indulged you. She cultivated your intellect. She made you the man you are.

"Will you tell me what the ogres are doing now? What their next move will be?"

"*This* is their next move, for now," Minith says. "After that, who knows? Why would they tell me?"

Isadora isn't expecting you to jump in one of your newly-acquired helicopters and fly to Hypatian, of course, deep within enemy territory. Instead, she proposes a meeting with just herself and a handful of servants, somewhere out in the open, neither under one set of guns nor the other. And it remains a risk, depending on just which of the Brink-era toys the ogre generals have got working. You have read about snipers and drone strikes and the like. But the risk would extend to her, and you respect the value that Isadora places on her own life. She lacks the infantile recklessness of your early conquests, the Masters who couldn't bring themselves to believe that their servants could ever be a credible threat.

Now you're a threat. Now they believe in you.

You confer with Roben and Bradwell and Layla and all your other lieutenants, both here and at the end of a radio. They don't like it, but they don't know Isadora. You listen to them, but in your head the matter is already decided. You want to see your former master again, one last time. You want to sit with her and talk as equals, before the curtain is run down on this whole doomed business.

You arrive at the appointed place at evening. You bring Minith; release her into her Mistress's care, because you know the gesture will be appreciated. Isadora has a folding table set out, big enough for two ogres and a weight of rich food. Her promised handful of servants are unpacking hampers and cold boxes – the latter gives you a sudden shiver, a flashback to the kitchen of your home from years before – and laying out a movable feast. And Isadora sits there, in a chair sufficient for her dimensions, and watches you thoughtfully.

She is just as you remember her: massive, ogrishly beautiful, sly in her smiling. Her eyes flash as Minith lights the candles.

"Torquell," she names you. "Or is it 'general' now?" Because you've made an effort, decorated your long coat with stolen medals. You take the chair opposite her and hear it creak slightly.

"Welcome to my bower," Isadora says. She's had a glass or two already, you reckon; a somewhat incongruous and impolitic ambassador for ogre-kind. "I think 'bower' is the word. All very *Midsummer Night's Dream*. You're looking well, Torquell." And there's a little twitch there that might have been a murdered impulse to get up and pat you on the head, like she used to. "You've grown," she adds. "Or perhaps you've just grown into who you were always supposed to be. Genetically speaking."

You realise you're barely having to look *up* into her face at all. And is it because she's slouching a little already, or have you actually become more massive, more *ogrish*, since you left her?

Her opening gambit: "My fellows are really not happy with you, Torquell."

It's such an understatement you blink at her. "Good?" you try.

"Believe me, they're currently putting more effort into hushing up the news than fighting you. Don't want to look fools in front of the others."

And you take this piece of unsolicited information and stow it away because, of course, what they're also doing is stopping the humans, their monkeys, finding out about just what humans can do. There are more ways this news can spread than amongst the Masters. You've been sending people out to spread it, after all.

"Torquell," Isadora says, around mouthfuls, "this can't go on."

You eat in silence, savouring the rich sauces and meats, eating what she does as a rough and ready protection against poisoning. But you trust her not to try that, you find. Isadora was always frank with you.

"I mean, you've done it." She signals, and Minith refills her glass. "You've finally got everyone's attention. You've taken over all of poor Peter's estates and then some. You've killed some people. You've interrupted manufacturing. And now you've inspired a full scale revolt within the army, a result I place entirely at the feet of those idiot generals of ours and their determination to treat their people like dirt. So, yes, you've succeeded, that far. But they can't let you succeed any further, Torquell. The problem with my peers is that, lacking challenges and with no limits save where they jostle elbows with each other, there's little impetus for change and growth. They just fall into their ruts of lording it over the Economics and indulging their idiot games and pleasures. You remember what it's like for *me*, don't you? Me, someone who actually wants to further the boundaries of human knowledge. And the filthy deals I had to make, the treatment I had to endure, just to get support and resources.

"But you, Torquell, have *changed* all that. You've woken them up at last. You're sitting at their gates with their soldiers, armed with their weapons. You're finally being taken seriously. And so they're looking at the rest of the pre-Brink war toys. The big ones. Soon enough they'll have remembered how to brew a tailored plague or launch a missile from halfway around the world and drop it on the very top of your skull with pinpoint accuracy. And turn all of Peter Grimes's former holdings into a wasteland where nothing will ever grow, and all your followers to ash. You know this to be possible."

You nod. You do.

"And nobody wants that. I mean, now it's got this far, a couple of the generals probably do, because they're idiots, but it's a waste of land and a waste of Economics, and the hole it leaves in all our systems will take a long time to patch up. And you'll be dead, and all your dreams with you. And *I* don't want that."

A raised eyebrow from you. Minith refills your glass, but you leave it on the table, even as Isadora downs most of hers the moment it's topped up. She is looking at you fondly, despite everything. And you think about the fringe benefits of what she's described, from her point of view. You wonder how ogre science might advance, now that you've kicked them hard enough on the ankle. Now you've woken them up.

"You know what you are. I assume that finally pushed you to run away." She looks hurt about that. "You didn't have to. I had… plans for you. Plans in our society. But you went back to the Economics, and look where we've got to. You should be proud of what you've achieved, really. Not that I should say that, but I almost feel proud for you. Heritage will out, as we geneticists say."

"You think I'm one of you."

"You are." Wide-eyed surprise that you'd even doubt it. "I did wonder if you were even a direct descendant, some miscegenation, even though the engineered differences between human and Economic are supposed to make that impossible. But having studied your genome, it's just genes doing gene things. Switching themselves back on at random rather than staying safely quiet." A wild wave of the wineglass that spills half its contents. "You'd be surprised how few genes are really involved." Her smile is brilliant. "You won't care, but having someone else I can actually *talk* to about this is quite the treat. Usually it's just Minith and the others. And they're…"

"Economics," you fill in.

Monkeys.

"And you're…"

"An ogre."

She laughs. "Torquell, *really*. A human. Unmodified. Original."

"Like they were from before the Brink."

"Exactly," and probably she's about to go on to another topic, but you have a question. It's not one you even knew to ask, back when you were studying at her feet. The other puzzles she set you were too all-consuming. You didn't look past them to the big hole in all the histories, the thing the ogres never mentioned. And, unmentioned, it became an un-thing, a non-event. And yet, the more you think about the Brink, and what was done to remake the bulk of the thronging population into something smaller and more Economic, the more you realise there is one question more that must be asked. And if anyone knows, Isadora will.

"What happened after the Brink?" you ask her.

She makes a vague gesture probably intended to describe the whole world. "You know what. This. And depressingly little changed in the generations after."

"No," you say, and you see the faintest guilty start in her face that tells you she knows what you mean. "*After* the Brink. After the last generation of original humans had passed on and there were just the Economics and the ogres. What happened then? Because something must have."

Now it's her turn to be silent and listen. You can feel a colossal weight of anger somewhere, circling like a drone weapon, waiting to see if it needs to drop on you and set you ablaze.

"Because the whole problem with the Brink," you go on slowly, step by logical step, "was that the world was overfull with people, all of them consuming too much, too inefficiently. That was why your ancestors ordered it all, the genetic engineering. Volunteers at first, then mandatory, and then camps. I've read the books. I know. Until everyone's children came out small and meek and vegetarian – except yours – and the world was saved." A deep breath. "Except the world was still full of people. Smaller people. Meeker people. Economics. But still full. Overfull, but even if everyone's smaller, the number of people is still the same or going up. And now." You mimic her gesture, taking in all the world. "Open fields, sprawling forest. And they cram them in, in the factory towns, but they don't *need* to. There's space for everyone to have their own farm. There's *wilderness*. Your peers go hunting and shooting and fishing. They have whole play-wars from horizon to horizon. There's so much space."

"What happened," you ask her, "to all the people?"

For a long time she says nothing. The ebullience is gone. She stares at the gleam of the candle as filtered through the gold of her glass's contents.

"It was generations ago now," she says quietly, and for a moment you can't understand why that's relevant. And it isn't relevant to you, but it is to her. She's trying to shed the blame of it. *I wasn't there.*

"When we'd made them smaller, and more docile," she tells you, so softly that you lean in to hear her, "there were still too many of them, as you say. The world was full of people. And history has a particular curve when it comes to numbers of people. There's a time, before industry and technology get going, when you *want* lots of people. If you're a king or a duke or something, you want people to till your fields and work your mines and march in your armies. Population is power, and nobody wants for work unless they're incurably idle. But then you get factories and automation and ways of doing things that are just more efficient than the old ways. Why have someone painstakingly carve out a chair over a month when ten unskilled hands in your factory can make a hundred chairs in the same time? And you keep automating and inventing ever more ingenious ways of doing things that don't need people, and eventually, if you're sitting at the top of the heap, you realise that all those teeming multitudes of people aren't actually an advantage. In fact, they're a positive drawback. You don't really *want* a vastly populous country, just in case those people all decided *they* don't want *you*.

"And of course by now there's very little for these people to do, and so you either have to spend half your time keeping them sufficiently amused that they won't realise they're pointless and have no purpose, or risk exactly the sort of stunt *you're* currently pulling, Torquell. So, back before the Brink we already understood that there really was no point to all those people. And afterwards they were small enough and weak enough and different enough that they couldn't stop us doing something about that. Remaking the world into something a bit more manageable. Where we" – and it's hard for her to say that *we,* but she is honest enough to force herself to it – "could get on with what we wanted to do. Without quite so many people underfoot."

And she looks at you, all cheer gone, watching for your reaction, Your face is flat and without expression, though, so the words keep falling out of her.

"It was mostly done through the release of chemical and biological agents, I think," she says faintly. "After all, there were distinct genetic markers separating us from the Economics. We could tailor things to lower reproductive rates, spread sterility. Humane, Torquell. And where it wasn't humane, I'm sure it was at least... quick." And that's all the words, the story as she knows it. She has the grace to be ashamed of it, but only distantly. The tilt of her chin says, *This was a long time ago. It's done. We have to get on with our lives.* As though her every waking moment hasn't benefitted from what was done back then. Her only saving grace is that she's not trying to tell you how the great open world of today is better for the monkeys than the tight-packed world of the Brink. And maybe it is, in some ways, but not for all the people who never got to see it.

"And..." you get out.

"And then we could live how we wanted. With the freedom of room and space, and fewer other people to worry about. Just as many people as we needed to play lord of the manor, or to fight wars, or to work in factories because it's cheaper and easier to have most factories run by Economics. Robots are expensive to build and fix and replace, and Economics are cheap and replace themselves. Everyone could indulge all the dreams they ever had, about how they'd act if they ruled the world."

"Everyone who wasn't an Economic," you clarify. The words echo inside you, in the great vacant pit of you. You're waiting to see what emotion will flood in and fill it.

"Yes."

"This," you try, "is why we have to fight." And it's not why you have been fighting, because you only just found out this new Truth, but it could be why you fight from now on. It could be part of your Truth going forwards. The banner under which your army marches.

"Torquell," Isadora says. "They won't let you."

A masterful raised eyebrow from you. They haven't stopped you yet.

"When it was just you overturning an apple cart out in the sticks, then it was something for people to jockey and compete over, a game for the more bored of the generals. It was the only kind of opportunity most of my peers have left: a chance to point out the flaws in other people's handling of a situation. Even when you killed a few people" – and she means *ogres*; she doesn't mean the Economics who died, in far greater numbers, during the fighting – "it was local and contained and, for most of us, rather far away. But if you try and change the order of the world then they'll just obliterate you. You can't win."

You take another mouthful of steak, though it's bitter with newfound knowledge. "So why come?"

"Because nobody wants to have to *use* those weapons – to destroy so much just to stop you."

"And because they blame you for making me?"

And she actually smiles. "No," she says. "They haven't quite put those pieces together." But you realise *she* believes she made you, with her library and the years she gave you when you could grow into the man you were meant to be. She takes credit, not blame. You're something fascinating, an experiment, and she is a scientist first and foremost. And you were always her favourite.

"But," she adds, "they did listen when I told them I had another solution. And they didn't like it, but it's better than burning everything down, and you have pushed them a long way. Far enough that concessions are on the table."

You lean forwards. You both do. Like lovers, almost. The lovers you always wondered if you might become, if she decided to impose herself on you. You had troubled dreams, surely, about just that, and sometimes they were bad dreams and sometimes they weren't.

"Concessions," you echo.

"You can have it," she says, almost a whisper. "What you've won. You can keep it. They'll let you."

"They'd never."

"They will," she insists. "You'll hold it like Sir Peter held it, though. As part of the system. Call it your birthright."

You jerk back, clutching for a derisive expression. "I lead their slaves in a revolt; I kill their people and burn their houses. And they welcome me with open arms? Is that what I'm supposed to believe?" And you probably don't quite notice that, for the purpose of the conversation, you are not one of 'the slaves' and Isadora is not one of 'them.' You're outside the world, the two of you, in the little bubble of your bower.

"No, listen," Isadora is saying, and hurriedly, before you do anything rash. Because she actually cares, you realise. Not about the Economics, not about the social order. About what happens to you, her stray pet turned barbarian warlord. "They will accept it. Not happily, and don't expect to get invited to many parties or anything, but if you just take on that mantle, recast your conquests from revolution to... hostile takeover, let's say. Become the squire of the manor, and you can keep it all. The people who came to your banner, the land you currently hold, even the factories and the city. Treat people well, be a benevolent master to them, make what changes you want, to make their lives easier. Maybe you can even show that things are more efficient that way. You might start a trend. You'll have a friend in me, to argue your case, if you can show results. You can even keep the weapons – you have no idea how many times I've patiently told rooms full of idiot men how asking you to give them up wouldn't exactly build trust. But don't push any further. No more conquests, no more fomenting rebellion amongst other people's Economics. You have won a lot, Torquell. Yours isn't the first rebellion since the Brink, by any means, but it's the most successful, hands down. Be happy with what you've achieved."

"They won't let it lie," you hear yourself say. "Unless we keep moving forwards, they'll regroup and then they'll destroy us."

"No." She shakes her head, and that little smile is still there, proud of you. "I mean, if you were just a mon– just an Economic who'd cooked all this up, then they *couldn't* make this kind of offer. That's a boundary nobody's about to cross. It's unthinkable. But you're not one of them, Torquell. You're one of us. An... 'ogre,' if you will. A real human being, with all the appetites and drives humans were supposed to have. How else have you achieved so much so quickly? Born to rule, Torquell. Destined for it. Now join the company of your peers, where you were always supposed to be. Be the most benevolent and progressive master the world ever saw. Show us all how it's done, but do it as one of us." And that bubble bursts, and she's 'us' again, and you are standing with one foot either side of that unbridgeable divide.

And you think. You take a long time because there is much to be said on both sides. Security for the people you've freed. A light hand, a better life, a master who won't be a petty tyrant like Sir Peter or a great butchering monster like the generals were. You could take up that mantle of authority and not be corrupted by the power, you're sure.

And a betrayal, you must realise. But there are many factors here, and you believe Isadora. You and she could enjoy many meals like this, afterwards, as you discussed how to improve the world and save it from its problems. Just like her distant ancestors did, as they approached the Brink.

You have worked so hard since you left her house. And your destiny has two paths now. The one where all that fighting was the prelude to a greater fight, a war for the whole world; then the one where all that fighting went to earn you this, and no more. But *This* is still more than you ever thought they'd let you keep.

"Yes," you tell her, and a great weight falls from you. The weight of fear, that any given morning will see your little uprising quashed by the monstrous weapons of the Brink days. The weight of responsibility that you'll get all your followers killed. The weight of worry that you might *lose;* that you might be *humiliated*. That the ogres would haul you down to the dirt and make you crawl before they killed you.

But they reserve that fate for monkeys, and you are, by genetic fluke, an ogre.

Isadora's eyes sparkle and her smile spreads, and Minith is conjured forward to refill the glasses, and you toast your new agreement. The wine is sweet again, the taste of ashes gone. You're already thinking through what you will say to your lieutenants, how this is not a capitulation, barely even a concession. A victory! Safety and prosperity for all! They can go back to their farms and factories knowing they won, and honestly, how many revolutionaries throughout history can ever say that?

Isadora belches, smirks, a hand halfway to her lips. Only halfway, though. Her face is oddly set. Guttering candlelight glimmers on the sweat of her brow.

"I…" Her lips move, but there's no more.

You are very still, watching her. Not by design. Your muscles slow. Your lungs labour. It's quick acting, the agent, but that's the advantage of living in a great house admirably equipped with laboratories.

I watch you die.

I watch you die, Torquell. You, the hero, who achieved so much, so effortlessly. And afterwards, I and the other servants pack everything away, and I consider how best to get word to your people to tell them you were betrayed. Their great hero was murdered at the feast, and they must rise up, rise up. Spread the word far and wide that the ogres cannot be trusted. Spread the Truth of what was done to their ancestors; Torquell's Truth, we can call it. And I will midwife your legacy. I will make you a true hero, mythic in your grandeur. It's always easier when you're dead.

And you could have said 'No.' I wanted you to say no. I know you always felt I hated you, but believe me, I was very invested in you and your potential. For years I made sure the right books were under your hand when you reached for them; the answers rose to your eyes when you sought them. Isadora thought she made you, but if anyone brought Torquell the Hero into the world it was poor, unassuming Minith.

And for years before that, I built up my networks, little cells of people taking to other cells and nobody knowing the whole. A system I inherited from others and built upon, carrying my own private business everywhere Isadora took me. I primed Bradwell and the others in the army, showing them the injustice of their lot and readying them for the coup. I liaised with the disgruntled shop stewards of the factory workers and talked about strikes and go-slows and protests. I primed the world to be ready for a figurehead like you, a man who would set a match to all the tinder I had shored up about the place. And you brought the match, and for as long as it lasted, your career as a revolutionary was glorious. Just what we needed.

Then came Isadora with her offer, and you could have said 'No.'

I'll miss Isadora. She was the best ogre I ever knew. She was a kind Mistress, and she had a brilliant mind, and she reserved her spite and anger for her own peers, who smothered her and kept her down because ogres, on the whole, tend not to like ogresses who get above themselves. But when you're property, it doesn't matter if your owner treats you well or badly. The ownership is all. We don't split hairs about who is a better slave master. And you would have been the best owner of all, and that still isn't enough reason to keep you alive once you've decided that owning people is fine, just so long as it's *you* that owns them.

So now you're a dead hero, and that's useful too. Your movement and its momentum are still very much alive, and I will keep working behind the scenes to spread the word and the fire. Because it's *on*, now. It's us or them. And we have an army and weapons, and they have an awful lot of servants and workers and soldiers, and they don't know who they can rely on, and there aren't enough of *them* to do it all themselves. They're very used to having things done for them. They have the power now, and the strength, and the long-held habits of command, but we will keep lighting fires and teaching the Truth. Until the whole world is burning, and all the masters are gone.